Shades of Murder

A Mac Faraday Mystery

By

Lauren Carr

Shades of Murder

For information call: 304-285-8205
or Email: writerlaurencarr@comcast.net

Designed by Acorn Book Services

Publication Managed by Acorn Book Services
www.acornbookservices.com
info@acornbookservices.com
304-285-8205

ISBN-13: 978-0985726706
ISBN-10: 0985726709

Printed in the United States of America

To My Beloved Family

Shades of Murder

Cast of Characters
(in order of appearance)

David O'Callaghan: Spencer police officer, promoted to chief of police after death of his father, Police Chief Patrick O'Callaghan. Mac Faraday's half-brother.

Police Chief Patrick O'Callaghan: Spencer's legendary police chief. The love of Robin Spencer's life.

Archie Monday: Personal assistant to world-famous mystery author Robin Spencer. Lives in the guest cottage at Spencer Manor.

Robin Spencer: Queen of Mystery. World famous mystery author. Upon her death, it is revealed that as a teenager she had a son out of wedlock, to whom she has left her vast fortune. She is the love of Police Chief Patrick O'Callaghan's life.

Arthur Bogart: Spencer's Deputy Police Chief. Best friend of Patrick O'Callaghan. David's godfather.

Neal Hathaway: Multi-millionaire and CEO of Hathaway Industries, which builds and launches satellites.

Greta: Neal Hathaway's housekeeper.

Susan Dulin: Neal Hathaway's executive assistant.

Rachel Hathaway: Neal Hathaway's daughter-in-law. Married to Scott Hathaway.

Ilysa Ramsay: Artist. Neal Hathaway's wife.

Reggie: Package Delivery Service Trainee.

Kevin: Package Delivery Service Driver.

Gnarly: Mac Faraday's German Shepherd. Only dog to be dishonorably discharged from the United States Army. Don't ask them why. They refuse to talk about it.

Mac Faraday: Underpaid homicide detective. His wife leaves him and takes everything. On the day his divorce became final, he inherited $270 million and an estate on Deep Creek Lake from his birth mother, Robin Spencer.

Archibald Poole: Millionaire Art Collector.

Peyton Kaplan: Vice-President in charge of security at Hathaway Industries.

Nancy Kaplan: Peyton Kaplan's wife.

Victor Gruskonov: Ilysa's business manager.

George Scales: Neal Hathaway's lawyer.

Joshua Thornton: Hancock County, West Virginia, prosecuting attorney, former JAG lawyer. Retired after the sudden death of his wife Valerie left him to raise five children on his own. He is looking forward to a relaxing two-week vacation as an empty-nester—until he agrees to do a favor for the last person he expected to do a favor for.

Reverend Brody: Prison pastor. Friend of Joshua Thornton.

Oliver Cartwright: Serial Rapist and Murderer. Serving life in prison.

Lieutenant Sherry Bixby: Head of Homicide Division with Pennsylvania State Police stationed in Pittsburgh barracks.

Detective Cameron Gates: Pennsylvania State Police's top homicide detective. She had investigated the Oliver Cartwright murders.

Irving: Cameron Gates's cat. You'd have issues too if you looked like a skunk.

Priscilla Garrett: Senior Forensics Technician.

Admiral: Joshua Thornton's dog. The Irish Wolfhound-Great Dane mix has the heart of a chicken.

Special Investigator Harry Bush: FBI agent. He has one more case he wants to close before he retires.

Investigator Kenny Hill: FBI agent, training to replace Harry Bush, if he can survive this last case.

Jeff Ingles: Spencer Inn's nervous manager.

The one charm about marriage is that it makes a life of deception absolutely necessary for both parties.

Oscar Wilde

Shades of Murder

Prologue

Deep Creek Lake, Maryland - September 6, 2004

"—and in other news…On Friday, prosecutors wrapped up their side in the murder trial for Oliver Cartwright in Pittsburgh, Pennsylvania.—"

While the radio announcer read off the morning report, David O'Callaghan poured his first cup of coffee. He dumped one spoonful of sugar into his oversized United States Marine Corps mug, a graduation gift from an old girlfriend, bestowed to him upon completing officers training.

The mug lasted longer than the girlfriend.

Taking his first sip of coffee, he gazed out the kitchen window of his parent's cozy lakeshore house to admire the leaves flapping on the birch trees lining the shore. When he squinted his eyes, he could see a hint of gold on the tips of the leaves.

Tomorrow would be his day off to celebrate Labor Day. While everyone else was celebrating it today proper, he would be trying to keep them from killing themselves, or each other, around Deep Creek Lake.

The radio continued with the news at the top of the seven o'clock hour.

"—Lawyers for Cartwright will begin presenting their defense on Tuesday. Oliver Cartwright has confessed to raping and killing six women in and around the Pittsburgh area during the summer of 2003."

Six? David brought the mug to his lips for another sip. *I could have sworn Cartwright killed seven women. Where did I hear it was seven?*

The ring of the phone broke through the chirping of the birds in the birch trees. David didn't realize he was still half asleep until the hot drink splashed onto the breast of his white shirt. Cursing, he slammed down the mug to send more coffee spilling across the kitchen counter.

"Damn it!" He grabbed the dish towel to mop up the coffee from his shirt. The phone was still calling out to him while he wiped off his silver police shield.

"Coming!" He grabbed the phone and braced it against his ear with his shoulder while wetting the dish towel to continue the cleanup.

"Did I wake you?"

Hearing the lilt of Archie Monday's voice coming through the phone line transformed his morning into a good day. Forgetting about the coffee, David stood up straight. "No. You're up early."

"I wanted to catch you before you went to work. Robin wants to know if you're coming over for steaks on the grill after you get off."

That's a no-brainer.

David stepped into the half-bath off the kitchen to check his reflection in the mirror. He ran his hand over his blond hair. *She's on the phone, you dummy.* He went back to dabbing at the coffee on his shirt.

"Are you still there?" she asked him.

"Yeah."

This isn't going to work. After tossing the dish towel into the sink, he proceeded to unbutton his shirt.

"Let me think." David slammed open the bedroom door in his search of a clean shirt. "Thick juicy steaks hot off the grill at Spencer Manor with two of the loveliest ladies on Deep Creek Lake, or hot dogs zapped in the microwave and a can of beer? What do you think?"

The sound of her laughter almost made him forget about his disgust over the dirty shirt. "What time should we expect you?"

"I get off at six."

"Wonderful. Bring your swim trunks. We'll go jet skiing," she said.

Which means I'll see you in your swimsuit.

David paused in his search for a clean shirt to imagine Robin Spencer's stunning assistant in a bathing suit. It was something he had been yearning for since meeting Archie Monday.

A stern tone in her voice brought him back down to earth. "I should warn you. Robin's working on a plotline that involves Marine Special Forces. Be prepared for an interrogation."

Pushing the vision of Archie in a bikini from his mind, David shifted the phone from one ear to the other while shrugging out of his shirt. "Ah, so she's using me."

"What can I say?" Her tone was cool. "She's a woman. We all use men."

"Won't be the first time I've been used by a woman." It sounded like she was about to hang up when David stopped her. "What can I bring tonight?"

"Just your handsome self."

He stopped her again. "Dad tells me that you're a wine expert."

He could hear the laughter in her voice when she replied, "I wouldn't say I was an expert. Robin knows more about it than I do. But I'm learning. We're working on expanding the Spencer Inn's wine list. So we've been doing a lot of wine tasting lately. This week, we received a case from Burma. We'll test it out tonight."

"Now, I'm intimidated. I was going to offer to bring the wine tonight."

"You can never miss with a good cabernet sauvignon."

Making a mental note to stop by the wine shop to pick up a good bottle of red wine—not the cheap stuff—*You don't serve the cheap stuff to one of the world's most famous mystery writers and her beautiful assistant*—David finished dressing for the second time that day. He strapped on his utility belt with his gun, radio, baton, and cell phone.

Before slipping on his mirrored sun glasses to block out the bright morning rays reflecting off the water, David O'Callaghan paused to admire the platinum blond streaks that the sun and lake water had added to his already light hair. With his face and body bronzed after a summer of working and playing on the water, he looked even blonder than usual.

After taking a quick glance around the house to make sure everything was secured and put away, he stepped outside onto the front porch and locked the door.

Leaving an empty house was not part of his usual routine. His mother was always home during the day, but today was different. His parents had left two days before for a vacation at the Grand Canyon.

That was something else that was out of the ordinary. In all of his twenty-four years, David didn't recall his parents ever going away together, anywhere, for anything. Police Chief Patrick O'Callaghan would travel to conferences or training, or his mother would check in to the hospital when she'd get sick.

Vacation? Together? What brought that on? Maybe Robin knows.

"Hey, kid!"

Startled, David dropped his keys in the driveway. Out on the road, Police Officer Art Bogart laughed from the front seat of his cruiser. On his way to the station, where he was acting as Spencer's chief, he had pulled off the road to give David a good-natured hassling.

Bogie was the oldest, and most respected, member of Spencer's small police force. With the size and condition of a body builder, he had been challenged more than once by a cocky rookie, only to put the youngster in his place by pinning him to a mat in less than thirty seconds. In contrast to his size and strength, a heart of gold beat behind his silver shield.

"You going to work or not? Your daddy's away, so you decided to play around and be late?"

David knelt down to pick up the keys. "I'm coming. I had to make sure everything was locked up."

"Well, get your butt in gear, son!" Bogie called out to him from across the driver's compartment of his cruiser. "There was an accident last night. We have a car that hit a deer on Spencer Lane, rolled, and landed in the lake."

"Any fatalities?"

"So far we have a six-point buck. Miracle if the driver made it. No witnesses. A couple of runners found the car this morning." He waved his arm at him. "Get a move on! Two-point-three miles down Spencer Lane toward Pelican Court. The divers should be there already."

Bogie hit the gas pedal so hard that the tires spit gravel when he pulled out to speed down the road like he was trying to merge into rush hour traffic. On the shores of Deep Creek Lake, among the Shenandoah Mountains, he was only dealing with the rush minute.

David climbed into his police cruiser to head in the opposite direction, along the tree-lined shore road, to take him to the scene of the accident.

On Labor Day, the seasonal residents along the lake were waking up to enjoy the last breath of summer before closing up their vacation homes for winter. Meanwhile, up at the top of the mountain overlooking the lake, behind the scenes, the Spencer Inn was gearing up for snow season to start in eight weeks.

Thoughts of Spencer Inn made David's mind wonder to that of its owner, Robin Spencer, a good family friend, which brought his mind back to that of Archie Monday.

The green-eyed blond had come to work for Robin Spencer while he was serving in Afghanistan. They had only met briefly after he had returned from overseas, before going off to the police academy. Now that he was back home, he considered the possibilities.

I wonder if Archie Monday likes men in uniform. Robin'll certainly put in a good word for me. David made a mental note to call the restaurant manager at the Spencer Inn. *He'll know what wine would impress Archie.*

Bogie's voice burst from his radio to jar David back to reality. "Change of plans, kid! Go to the Hathaway Estate on Pelican Court instead. I'll send Fletcher to take care of the car accident."

David snatched the mike from the radio. "What's at Hathaway's estate?"

"They got a DB, kid. Dead body."

David flipped the switch for the lights and sirens and pressed his foot on the gas pedal.

⚃ ♏ ☒ ♏

Neal Hathaway's summer home was the only residence on Pelican Court, a secluded lane that crossed a mountain stream to cut through some thick woods. A rarely used entrance to the state park marked the other end of Pelican Court. Anyone not curious enough to travel the lane would never notice the mansion hidden behind the thick grove of trees.

The owner and CEO of Hathaway Industries lived behind a brick wall and iron gates with a brass "H" marking them. The estate's driveway snaked down a landscaped hill to the stone house that had one of the best views on the lake.

David O'Callaghan had encountered more than his share of exposure to murder investigations. With his father being chief of police, and working with the military police in the Marines, he had been called to more than one crime scene that involved a homicide.

Such scenes had an atmosphere of somberness. Everyone, including the investigating officers, would speak in soft tones with an air of respect for those who had passed on.

This, however, was the first time that David had been called to the scene of a dead body at a multi-millionaire's estate.

During the short time it took him to drive around the lake to the Hathaway Estate, David tried to recall what he knew about Neal Hathaway.

Self-made millionaire. Always wanted to be an astronaut. Was also a science geek. When he failed to become an astronaut, he used his talent for science and rocketry to build what was now a Forbe's Top 100 company. Hathaway Industries was one of the government's biggest contractors for launching and maintaining defense satellites. They were also in the race to become the first to offer private flights into outer space.

Neal Hathaway was indeed a real live rocket scientist.

Other than that, David was unsure about anything else. *Guess I'm going to find out now.*

David drove through the gates and pulled his cruiser around to a multi-car garage with a black SUV parked in front of it. The lights and the sirens failed to break up the fight taking place next to the vehicle.

Two women were rolling on the ground with their hands in each other's hair. Judging from the disheveled condition of their clothes and the exhausted grunts they uttered between their high-pitched curses, David surmised the fight had been going on for a while.

With a head full of curly platinum blond hair that looked like a mop, one of the women appeared to be on the losing end of the fight. The shoulder strap of the blonde's white dress had been ripped off to expose her voluptuous breast. The rest of her garment wasn't in a much better condition. The side seam had been ripped wide open to show a white girdle.

Even though she was winning, the blond's opponent wasn't in much better shape. During the course of the battle, her bright purple mini skirt had been pulled all the way up her hips to reveal that her underwear consisted of a black thong.

Several feet away, a woman dressed in a housekeeper's uniform, was pleading for them to stop. When David brought his car to a stop, she yelled over the siren in a thick European accent. "Help, please! They're going to kill each other."

Turning off the lights and siren, David threw open the car door. "Okay, that's enough. Break it up."

Not seeming to notice him, they continued wrestling with their fingers entwined in each other's hair.

"Give it back," the brunette in the purple skirt grunted in an exhausted voice.

"No!"

"I said to break it up!" David rushed over to where they were fighting.

The brunette rolled over to straddle the blond and slapped her face repeatedly.

David reached down to grab the brunette around the waist and lifted her off the other woman. Screaming in a high pitch, she twisted in his arms in an attempt to break loose. As soon as she was free, the blond jumped up to her feet and charged to swing her fist at her assailant's face. As luck would have it, the brunette dodged the blow.

David wasn't so lucky. The blond's fist made direct contact with his nose. His sunglasses went flying.

The stars that burst before his eyes could only be described as multi-colored brilliance. He swore he could even hear the fireworks explode inside his head. Later, he would recall with pride that even while he was stumbling after the assault that had broken his nose, which caused blood to splatter all over his white shirt, he did not lose sight of the matter at hand. Even as he was staggering around the driveway while trying to shake off the blow, he still kept hold of the brunette, who was struggling to get back into the fight.

The explosion of pain inside his head was amplified by the blast of an air horn behind him.

The brunette stopped struggling.

The women stopped shrieking.

Even the ringing in David's ears subsided in obedience to the air horn.

"Now that I have everyone's attention," David heard Bogie call out from somewhere behind him. "I believe someone called 9-1-1 about a dead body."

Like a student in a classroom answering a question, the housekeeper raised her hand. "That would be me," she said with a thick accent. "It's Ms. Ramsay." She pointed up over their heads to a second floor above the garage. "Mr. Hathaway found her in her studio. Someone …" She choked. "…killed her."

"I think you can put her down now." Bogie stepped over to where David was still holding the brunette up off the ground with his arms around her waist. "Are you going to behave, Miss?"

For her answer, the brunette glared over at the blond.

While he retrieved his sunglasses from the grass, and a handkerchief from the cruiser to hold on his nose, David noticed that the blond was older than he had first thought. The thick nest of blond curls and voluptuous build were misleading. Up close, her face revealed lines under heavy makeup.

"She started it," the brunette pointed at the other woman. "She was trying to make a run for it."

"I was not," the blond said. "I was getting my car ready to go." She told the two officers. "I have an important meeting in Pittsburgh tomorrow that I have to get ready for. Mr. Hathaway said I could leave as soon as I give the police my statement."

David asked, "And you are—"

"Susan Dulin. Neal Hathaway's executive assistant." With one hand, she tugged up on what was left to the shoulder of her dress, while adjusting her white high-heeled sandals with the other. With every move, her nest of platinum spirals spilled into her face and over her shoulders.

Seeming to notice David's handsome form for the first time, the brunette pulled down her skirt and smoothed her hair. "I'm Rachel." She held out her hand to him. "I hope you don't think I'm a nut, but Susan was trying to get away; and I know that when it comes to crimes like this, the police need to question everyone." She flashed him a grin. "I used to be a journalist."

With a wicked grin, Susan said, "Rachel is married to Scott, Neal's son."

Rachel shot her a glare, which Susan returned with equal hostility.

While David made notations in his notepad, Bogie called over the housekeeper who was watching them from the other side of the SUV. "What's your name?"

"Greta." She cast her eyes down to the ground.

"What can you tell us?" Bogie asked her.

"Nothing," she said. "I was cooking breakfast when Mr. Hathaway called on the intercom, and told me that his wife was dead and to call the police. After I called you, I came out here to wait."

"Where is he?" David asked.

"He's up there with her." She pointed again to the upper-level of garage.

"I guess we need to go see Mr. Hathaway." Noticing the bloody nose, Bogie asked, "What happened to you?"

David wiped his nose and examined the thick, sticky red substance on his handkerchief. The bleeding was letting up. "I got sucker punched."

"By a girl." Bogie's broad shoulders shook with laughter. "I can't wait to tell your pa about that."

The older officer's radio crackled. "Hey, Bogie?"

Pressing the handkerchief to his nose, David leaned his head back to stop the bleeding.

"Yeah, Fletcher?" Bogie answered with a laugh in his voice.

"We got a problem with this car in the lake," the officer reported. "The driver's dead. It's a rental car checked out by a Charles Smith at Dulles Airport yesterday. He's got a Miami, Florida, address. Problem is that Charles Smith is alive."

They exchanged glances. "What's that?" asked Bogie into the radio.

Fletcher explained, "I called the phone number that the rental car company has for Charles Smith. A guy answered. He's Charles Smith. He says that someone stole his identity months ago, and he's been trying to straighten it out since forever. When I told him this dude was dead, he said 'Good'." The officer asked, "What do you want me to do? We have nothing to tell us who this guy really is."

David cracked, "Maybe the real Charles Smith killed him."

Hearing him, Fletcher's voice came over the radio, "It wasn't a homicide. At least, I don't think it was. The buck killed him." He chuckled. "The buck that killed him is dead, too. I guess we could call it a murder-suicide."

Bogie said, "Get this guy's fingerprints and run them through AFIS. If he's an identity thief, maybe he's in the system."

When they climbed the stairs to the floor above the garage, David and Bogie could hear wrenching sobs coming from inside the room that appeared to be a studio apartment. The door leading into the studio was ajar.

Unsure exactly what would be waiting for them inside, they both placed their hands on their guns. Bogie eased the door open and stepped inside.

It was hard to believe that the sunny studio with a full view of the lake through the deck doors was now the scene of a bloody homicide. A kitchenette took up the far wall of the great room. A spiral staircase led upstairs to a loft.

The studio had canvases displayed on the walls and works in progress lined up on easels. Most of them were lake scenery or nature. Others were still life. A paint-covered smock lay across a stool resting before an empty easel.

On the floor, a man cradled the bloody body of a woman wrapped in a white terry-cloth bathrobe that matched his. "It's okay, baby," he assured her in a raspy voice while stroking the blood-soaked red curls from her face. "It's going to be okay."

The police officers exchanged somber expressions.

"Mr. Hathaway?" Bogie stepped into the room. He stopped in front of a hammer painted red with human blood.

"Sshh," Neal Hathaway looked up at them with swollen red-rimmed eyes. "She's okay. Ilysa's going to be okay. I'm a rich and powerful man. I can afford the best doctors in the world. We can fix this."

David cocked his head for a better view of the woman in the blood-soaked bath robe.

The mass of red curls were matted against the side of what used to be his wife's face. What had once been a human face had been pounded into hamburger made of meat and bone.

"I'm a rich man," Neal Hathaway sobbed while rocking his wife's body in his arms. "We can save her."

"Mr. Hathaway?" Greta startled David when she touched his arm. When she saw the sight her hands flew to her mouth. "Are you okay, Mr. Hathaway?"

Bogie held up his hand in a gesture for her to stop. "I'm sorry, you can't come in." He turned back to the grieving husband. "I'm sorry, Mr. Hathaway, but it's best if you let your housekeeper take you back to the main house. We'll take care of your wife."

"What are you going to do?" Without looking up, he continued to stroke her hair.

"We'll take good care of her," Bogie assured him.

Greta held out her hand to him. "Come with me, Mr. Hathaway. I'll take care of you. You'll see."

Bogie helped him to his feet. The housekeeper clutched his elbow. At the door, Neal Hathaway turned around to take one last look at his wife, who was lying like a rag doll tossed aside, in the middle of the art studio.

Tears came to David's eyes while he watched Neal Hathaway cling to the one thing he was unable to fix with his wealth and power.

There are still some things that all the money in the world can't buy.

Chapter One

Deep Creek Lake - Present Day

"Okay, Reggie, our next delivery is One Spencer Court. That's the stone and cedar place at the end of the point. " Kevin chuckled when he read the address off the clipboard.

First day on the job and he's got a delivery on Spencer Court. Hey, you gotta learn sometime.

"What's so funny?" The pimply-faced trainee glanced over at his supervisor, who was in the van's passenger seat.

With a smile, Kevin pointed up ahead. "Take the next right and cross the toll bridge over the cove. That'll take you onto Spencer Point"

"Toll bridge?"

"You'll see."

Reggie eased the van onto the narrow bridge to cross over the cove. The shoreline in this corner of Deep Creek Lake was the residence of some of the most luxurious homes in the area. The houses along the peninsula increased in grandeur up to the cedar and stone mansion that occupied the tip of Spencer Point. "Wow," he breathed.

"Stop!" Kevin shouted.

Reggie hit the brakes. The van stopped so fast that the packages in the back spilled off their shelves. The only one that stayed put was the six-by-five foot flat box out for delivery to Spencer Manor.

"Watch where you're going, kid."

Motionless, like a sentry on duty, a German Shepherd blocked the center of the road on the bridge. His gaze was directed at them.

"What's he doing?" Reggie whispered.

Kevin cleared his throat. "Looks like he's sitting to me."

The young man looked on either side of the dog to judge if there was enough space to drive around him. There wasn't.

"What're you going to do?" the trainer asked.

"Honk my horn? That'll make him move." After Kevin shrugged his shoulders, the driver tapped the horn.

Without so much as a blink of his eyes, the dog didn't move in response to the blast. When the driver hit the horn repeatedly, the German Shepherd remained frozen in his spot in the road. Reggie pressed his palm to the horn and kept it there.

"Hey, cut it out!" an old man with a fishing pole yelled from a dock. "You're scaring the fish."

Reggie turned back to the canine cocking his head at him. The delivery man could swear he saw the dog's lips curl in a smirk. "I'm driving through. He'll jump out of the way."

"What if he doesn't?" asked Kevin.

"His fault if he's too dumb to jump out of the way of a moving vehicle."

"That's Gnarly," the trainer warned him. "He's a lot of things, but dumb isn't one of them. He's Mac Faraday's dog."

"Who?"

"Mac Faraday owns Spencer Manor." Kevin pointed to the end of the Point. "Nice guy, but I guarantee you, you run over his dog, and Faraday complains to the home office; then you'll be delivering packages to Pakistan."

"What am I supposed to do?"

"Make him to move."

Reggie threw open the door and walked over to the dog blocking the road. "Move it." He waved his arms. "Get out of here. Go home."

The shepherd remained rooted in the spot.

The skinny delivery man called back to his trainer. "He didn't even blink."

Chuckling at the sight, Kevin climbed out of the van. "He doesn't."

Reggie asked, "Does he bite?"

"He'll kill you if he has to."

Reggie peered down at the dog that he guessed to be the largest German Shepherd he had ever seen up close. His brown face was trimmed in silver. The thick fur that made up his mane was sable. His tall ears stood erect. If he wasn't such a nuisance, Reggie would think he was a beautiful animal. "You wouldn't bite me." He reached out to grab his collar. With a growl, Gnarly bared his teeth. Reggie jumped back.

"Told you he'd kill you if he had to." Kevin laughed.

"Then you make him move."

The trainer slipped a hand into his breast pocket. Stepping up to the dog, he held out his open palm to display a dog biscuit. "There you go, Gnarl."

After taking the biscuit, the German Shepherd trotted off the bridge and up a path leading into the woods.

With a laugh, Kevin turned to his trainee. "I told you it was a toll bridge." He climbed back into the van. "Let's go. We need to get this package to Mac Faraday."

CB   EO   CR   EO

The late Robin Spencer loved her gardening as much as she loved murder mysteries. The grounds of her homestead, known as Spencer Manor, displayed her green thumb in multi-colored glory.

While Mac Faraday took after his mother in many ways, gardening wasn't one of them. He didn't know the difference between a petunia and a dandelion; nor would he notice the rhododendron bushes calling out for food and water after a couple of days without rain.

It wasn't that Mac was a neglectful homeowner. He was diligent about giving Gnarly his six o'clock biscuit. He wasn't quite so conscientious when it came to tending to his late mother's gardens. He would be if the rhododendron bush jumped up and down on his chest at the morning's first light.

For that reason, Archie Monday had made it her personal mission to keep Robin Spencer's beloved gardens flourishing.

It had been a busy spring for the editor and research assistant. When she wasn't cooped up inside her stone cottage working on an upcoming release from a hot new writer, she was up to her armpits in mulch and plant soil.

It seemed as if God sensed that she needed a break. The day after she had sent off the book, the sun had risen to shine on Spencer Manor's gardens in full bloom. The estate resembled a floral rainbow of blues and reds and yellows.

In the guest cottage, Archie checked her reflection in the mirror and applied one more layer of blush to her cheeks. After combing every hair in her blond pixie cut in place, she covered it with a new hat.

She had compared notes with her best friend, Catherine Fleming, about the proper attire for the garden club luncheon at the Spencer Inn. This would be Archie's first meeting as a bona fide member of the same exclusive garden club, founded by Robin's grandmother. Archie wanted to make a good impression.

Spencer's own honest to goodness social debutante, Catherine Fleming had suggested a Chanel suit. She also recommended a hat to match. This season, hats were very in. In the sunshine yellow suit with a matching hat, Archie felt like a bumble bee. *I'm a cute one at least.*

After grabbing her matching yellow clutch bag, she locked the door to the guest cottage where she made her home and trotted up the stone path through the rose garden. She was climbing the steps to the manor's back deck when she heard the delivery truck roll through the stone entrance. Expecting the arrival of her new smart phone, she clasped the hat down tight on her head with her hand to keep it from flying off, and broke into a run to meet the truck.

There was no need to hurry. The delivery men were taking their time admiring the twenty-three foot spectacle occupying the far side of the circular driveway. Blue and white, the Cobalt speed boat rested on its trailer, while waiting for its new owner to launch her for her maiden voyage.

"Sweet," Kevin said while circling the boat. "Must be nice."

"Boys and their toys." Archie reached out to sign the tablet tucked under his elbow.

Kevin held the tablet out of her reach. "Sorry, Ms. Monday, but today we need the man's signature himself." He showed her an envelope that he had tucked underneath the tablet. "There's a letter for him, too. He's to sign for both of them."

Archie's face screwed up in puzzlement when she saw Reggie pulling the large package from the back of the truck. "I take it that's not my new phone." She hurried up the steps and went inside the mansion.

Kevin assisted his trainee in lifting the box from the back of the truck and carrying it up to the porch. "Do you remember Robin Spencer?"

"The writer? I remember us having to read some of her short stories in school. We saw a play that she wrote, too."

"She's the one that wrote all those books about the millionaire playboy named Mickey Forsythe—"

"I loved those Mickey Forsythe movies," Reggie said. "I didn't know they wrote books about him."

Kevin explained, "Mickey Forsythe was a cop who inherited millions of dollars. So he leaves the police force and goes around solving murders for kicks."

While they carried the box across the stone walk, the older man gestured with the toss of his head at the mansion. "After

Robin Spencer died last year, they found out that when she was a teenager, she had a baby out of wedlock. She left everything to him. That baby had grown up to be a big time homicide detective. Get it? Mac Faraday is the same guy his birth mother wrote about."

At the top step, the door opened. "I'm nothing like Mickey Forsythe." In contrast to the dark-haired super detective in leather jackets and dark glasses from Reggie's youth, the true life version of Mickey Forsythe wore jean cut offs, a faded blue shirt, and flip-flops on his feet.

"Yeah, right," Kevin chuckled. "And Gnarly is nothing like Diablo, Mickey Forsythe's German Shepherd."

"Are you talking about the dog that held us up at the bridge?" Reggie asked on their way across the threshold.

"Is Gnarly doing that again?" Archie directed them to carry the package down the three stone steps into the dropdown dining room on the other side of the living room.

Enthralled with being so close to one of his movie heroes, Reggie ignored the question. "I love Diablo." He handed the letter and tablet to Mac. "In that last movie, the bad guy tried to escape from Mickey by climbing up a ladder to the roof and Diablo actually climbed up the ladder and nailed the sucker."

"That's Gnarly all right." The older delivery man was laughing on his way back to the van. "There's nothing that dog can't do."

"What did you order?" Shaking her head, Archie stood in front of the package propped up against the backs of the dining room chairs. "Maybe it's a mattress."

Receiving no answer, she turned around to see that the front door was open. Perturbed that she would have to wait to find out what was in the box, she went outside in time to see Mac tearing out of the garage in his red Dodge Viper to follow the delivery van.

As the brown delivery van turned onto the bridge at the end of Spencer Court, Reggie's foot hit the brake once more when he found a hundred pounds of fur and teeth blocking the road. "Again?"

Kevin held out a dog biscuit to him. "You can't cross without paying the toll."

Reggie took the treat. "Wait until I tell my wife that I got held up by Diablo. She's never going to believe it." He heard the squeal of brakes behind the truck. While stepping up to the dog, he turned around to see who was waiting behind them. *Whoever it is, he's got a sweet ride in a red convertible.*

"You're in big trouble, mister!"

Feeling like his insides had jumped out of his skin, Reggie dropped the biscuit to the ground. Whirling around, he threw up his arms and fists to defend himself against whoever it was that had rushed up behind him.

Gnarly scooped up the biscuit.

Mac Faraday was advancing. "Yes, I'm talking to you." He pointed at the German Shepherd attempting to swallow the spoils of his extortion in one gulp. "What have I told you about playing the troll on the bridge? Bad dog. Get in the car."

Instead of obeying, the dog barked in protest while standing his ground.

"Don't give me your lip." Mac pointed at the Viper. "Get in the car."

The dog replied with a snarling bark.

"Get in the car."

Gnarly's barks rose in volume.

"In the car! Now!"

Hanging his head, Gnarly scampered to the car.

After uttering a heavy sigh, Mac turned to the two delivery men, who had been watching the argument with their mouths hanging open. "I'm sorry, gentlemen. This won't happen again." He turned to go back to the sports car. "What are you—Hey! That's my iPod! Bad dog! Drop it!"

"He's right," Reggie said after returning to his seat in the van. "They're nothing like Mickey Forsythe and Diablo."

ᘓ ᘒ ᘔ ᘖ

"Bad dog!" Mac chased Gnarly inside the house. "Up to your room and don't come out. I want you to think about what you did."

Instead of galloping up the stairs to the master suite, Gnarly jumped up onto the loveseat in the living room. Like a defiant child, the dog returned his master's glare.

"Do what I say." Mac pointed up the stairs. "You heard me."

Still, Gnarly refused to move.

"I'll teach you who's boss."

When Mac grabbed him by the collar, Gnarly pulled away. Keeping hold, he wrestled with the dog until he had him in a headlock. The two of them landed on the floor and rolled across the carpet toward the stone fireplace.

"Will you stop playing with Gnarly and open this box?" Archie called up to them from the dining room. "I'm dying to know what's in it."

Declaring himself the victor, Gnarly jumped up onto the loveseat and plopped down with an "Umph" noise.

Archie slipped the sealed envelope that had come with the package into Mac's hand.

"Who said dogs are man's best friends?" He frowned when he read the return address on the envelope. It was from a lawyer's office. He asked the dog on the loveseat, "Are we being sued by another one of your victims?"

Gnarly snorted and shook so hard that the tags on his collar rattled.

"Since when do lawyers send huge packages special delivery to people they're suing?" Archie waved an arm in the direction of the box. "You read the letter. I'll open it to see what's inside." Without waiting for permission, she kicked off her shoes and went into the kitchen to retrieve scissors for cutting the cord and tape sealing it shut.

Gnarly galloped down the steps to sniff at the box that had invaded his home.

Meanwhile, Mac tore at the envelope, which contained a letter and another envelope. The inside envelope was addressed in blue script to Robin Spencer with the word *PERSONAL* printed in capital letters underneath her name.

"What does the letter say?" Archie came back in from the kitchen. With the scissors, she broke through the plastic cord wrapped around the box.

Mac was still reading the first letter. "It's a bunch of legal mumbo jumbo. This guy, Archibald Poole, died. He had left this to Robin Spencer. In the event of her death preceding his, it was to be passed on to her next of kin. Since that's me, I get it."

Archie stopped snipping. "Archibald Poole?"

Gnarly stopped sniffing.

"Did you know him?" He was breaking through the seal of the white envelope addressed to Robin.

"Creepy old man. One of those eccentric rich guys. He didn't make it all on the up and up. I think Robin remained friends with him because he was good material for her books. He lived in a big mansion up on top of a mountain in southern West Virginia."

Mac was only half paying attention. "He left Robin a painting."

With one end unsealed, Archie peered inside the box to see that the contents were wrapped in brown paper and padding.

Sitting on the top step leading down into the dining room, Mac read the letter out loud:

Dearest Robin,

If you are reading this, then I'm dead and you are now observing my gift to you. So, what do you leave to the girl who has everything? When that girl is Robin Spencer, it's a mystery.

You will find that I have left you an Ilysa Ramsay painting. That alone makes it worth a fortune. But, ah, my dear Robin, this is not just any Ilysa Ramsay painting. It is her lost painting.

You will recall that Ilysa Ramsay was brutally murdered on your own Deep Creek Lake in the early hours of Labor Day in 2004. At the same time, her last painting was stolen from her studio where her dead body was discovered. She had unveiled what she had declared to be her masterpiece to her family and friends the same evening that she was murdered.

Grasping the frame wrapped in packaging, Archie tugged at the painting to pull it out of the box while Mac continued reading:

> *Everyone in the art world has been searching for Ilysa Ramsay's last work of art. With only a handful of people having seen it; and no photographs taken of it before its theft; its value is priceless.*
>
> *As my good luck would have it, a month after her murder, my guy called me. He had been contacted by a fence representing someone claiming to have the painting and wanting to unload it. Being familiar with Ilysa Ramsay's work, I was able to authenticate it. Also, I had seen reports from witnesses who had described it as a self-portrait of Ilysa.*
>
> *As I write this letter, Ilysa's murder has yet to be solved. Nor do I know who had stolen the painting. It was sold to me by a third party.*
>
> *And so, my dear lovely Robin, I leave this task to you. Here is the painting that the art world has been searching for, for years, and a mystery of who stole it, along with who killed its lovely artist. Enjoy, as I know you will!*
>
> *My Love,*
> *Archibald Poole*

Her yellow suit droopy, Archie slapped her hat down on the dining room table, and ripped through the padding to reveal the painting of a red-haired woman lying across a lounge with a red and green clover pattern. She was dressed in an emerald gown with a ruby red choker stretched across her throat. Ruby red jewels spilled down her throat toward the bodice.

Gnarly sat on the floor at Mac's feet to gaze at the painting.

They studied the image together.

"Just what I always wanted," Mac said. "A stolen priceless painting with a dead body attached to it."

Chapter Two

"Where is it?" Deputy Police Chief Art Bogart almost shoved Mac out of the way in his rush through the front door to see the painting. Spying it in the dining room, he sprinted across the granite floors.

It took less than ten minutes for Spencer's deputy chief of police to arrive after Mac had called the station to ask about the cold case of Ilysa Ramsay on Deep Creek Lake.

Police Chief David O'Callaghan stopped on his way through the door to greet Gnarly in their usual manner. The German Shepherd planted his front paws on David's shoulders to lick his face.

David was the main reason Mac had moved to Deep Creek Lake after coming into his inheritance. Along with the millions of dollars and the estate, Mac had also inherited his mother's journal, which revealed that he had a half-brother by his birth father, Police Chief Patrick O'Callaghan. It was too late for Mac to have a relationship with his father, who had died from terminal cancer five years earlier; but it was not too late for Mac to form a warm friendship with his sibling.

"You have to excuse Bogie," David said after easing the dog's paws to the floor. "He was the lead investigator in Ramsay's murder. Dad and Mom were on vacation when she was killed." Casting an eye at where his deputy chief was examining the painting in the other room, he lowered his voice. "Bogie took it personally that he couldn't solve this murder."

"I'm surprised with it being such a big case, and here in Spencer, that Robin didn't get involved in the investigation," Mac asked.

He noticed David, Bogie, and even Archie, exchange quiet looks.

David cleared his throat. "Dad was diagnosed with cancer right before it happened. He broke the news after coming back from the Grand Canyon." He added in a soft voice, "Needless to say, Robin had other things on her mind at that time…We all did…maybe that's why the case went cold the way it did."

Bogie's voice boomed from the dining room. "Did that letter say anything about who he got the painting from?"

Archie answered by handing him the letters from both the lawyer and Archibald Poole. Bogie read them while Mac and David moved in to examine the painting.

"How much do you think this painting's worth?" Mac asked the question he had been wondering since reading the letter written to his mother.

"Plenty," David said, "Even if it turns out not to be Ramsay's last painting. If it is, it's worth a whole lot more than that."

"How was it stolen?" Mac asked.

David knelt to take a closer look at the woman in the emerald gown. "Do you even know who Ilysa Ramsay was?"

"Painter," Mac answered, "and she was a redhead."

"I've seen a lot of Ilysa Ramsay paintings," David said. "This is the only one that's a self-portrait. That also adds to its value."

"Who are those other people?" Archie asked.

While the red-haired woman was the center piece, there were other people placed at the outer edges or behind her. In the upper back corner of the canvas, a silver-haired woman in black plucked a harp with red-tipped fingers. Her expression was made more somber by a gaunt appearance that made her face resemble a skeleton.

"That's the maid playing the harp. I recognize her by the gray hair." David pointed at a man in a suit behind Ilysa standing over a voluptuous blonde seated at the grand piano. He peered down at her abundant cleavage while supposedly admiring a gold necklace from which hung a ruby heart. "That's Neal Hathaway's assistant, Susan Dulin, with his vice president in charge of security, Peyton Kaplan. With all the government contracts they do for defense satellites, security is a big thing at Hathaway Industries."

On the other side of the canvas, a young couple drank champagne. David recognized the woman as Rachel Hathaway, and the man as her husband, Scott. Rachel fingered her diamond necklace while casting a glare at Susan and Peyton Kaplan.

Bogie was nodding his head. "Rachel's a gold digger if I ever saw one."

Archie said, "Everyone in this painting is a suspect."

"Nah!" Bogie argued, "She painted it before she was murdered."

"Archie's right. All of our suspects are in this painting." David pointed to a slender man with a goatee sipping from a china cup. His long hair was tied back at the base of his neck. "Based on the pictures we have of him, that's Victor Gruskonov."

Mac asked, "Who's Victor Gruskonov?"

"Ilysa's business manager," Bogie grumbled. "A person of interest."

Mac asked about another couple on the opposite side of grand piano from the assistant and vice president. Their drinks rested on top of the piano. They were looking over their shoulders at Ilysa. The woman's black hair, styled in a bob, was mixed with silver strands cascading over her head like a spider web. The lips of her wide mouth were painted red to match the color on her long fingernails. Between the spider web covering her hair and her blood red lips and nails, she reminded Mac of a creature from a horror film

"The woman is Nancy Kaplan," Bogie said. "Peyton's wife. The man is Neal Hathaway's lawyer George Scales."

Mac wondered, "Why isn't she with her husband? Ilysa has her on the other side of the piano with another man."

"Unfortunately," David said, "the artist isn't here to ask."

"Do you notice who's missing?" Archie asked them.

Bogie nodded his head. "Her husband. Neal Hathaway isn't in this painting."

David said, "Interesting. She painted everyone in her life, but not her husband."

"Could it be a forgery?" Archie asked.

Mac's heart sank at the vision of an unexpected windfall flying out the window.

"I doubt that," Bogie said, "Archibald Poole knew art. As a matter of fact, I questioned him after the murder. The little bastard was known to collect stolen pieces of art for his own private collection. I had a good idea that whoever stole it would have sold it to him." He waved the letters in his hands. "Damn it. I was right all along. He did have it."

Mac asked, "Could he have been connected to Ramsay's murder?"

"Poole wasn't into murder." David stood up and stepped back from the painting. "Ilysa Ramsay was married to Neal Hathaway. They lived lakeside on Pelican Court."

Mac asked, "The rocket scientist?"

"They had only been married a couple years at the time of the murder," David said. "She was making a name for herself in Europe when they met. Hathaway married her and brought her to the states and financed her career. He's a big patron of the arts. He introduced her to all the right people. She was on her way to becoming famous here in the States. She had a huge showing at the Louvre in Paris for October, but she was killed four weeks before her showing."

"What about the painting?" Mac asked.

David said, "Ilysa finished it the day before her murder."

Bogie explained, "She was superstitious. She was from Scotland and believed in all that superstitious stuff. She wouldn't show her work to anyone until it was done. She refused to even talk about a work in progress. She had finished the painting on Saturday, and unveiled it to her friends and family after dinner on Sunday night."

David said, "She had a houseful of guests because of the Labor Day holiday."

"This painting was supposed to be her center piece at the showing," Bogie said, "but when her husband found her body Monday morning, it was gone."

"The value of this painting doubled when she was murdered," Archie said. "That alone is a big motive."

Bogie's mustache twitched. "Which is why the first one I wanted to question was Victor Gruskonov, Ramsay's manager. Ilysa told Hathaway that she was quitting Gruskonov. She was heard arguing with him over the phone. He supposedly said he was coming out to talk to her. Then, she ends up dead." His eyes narrowed to slits. He uttered a growl deep in his throat that caused Gnarly to lift his head from where he had been resting it on top of Archie's feet. "Gruskonov was at the top of my list before and he still is."

"Problem is," David told Mac, "Victor Gruskonov hasn't been seen since before the murder."

Archie said, "That makes him look guilty to me."

"Me, too." Bogie was nodding his head so fast that it resembled a bobble.

Mac was studying the canvas that took up the length of his dining room table. "If he represented such a great artist, then his bread and butter were his connections in the art world. He couldn't just drop off the face of the earth and still survive."

"That's what you'd think," Bogie said. "As big as Ilysa was in Europe before marrying Hathaway, Gruskonov didn't need anyone else. Everyone knows he's wanted for this murder, and everyone has been on the lookout for him."

David told them, "According to his passport, he was in Germany at the time of the murder, but no one saw him since days before Ilysa was killed."

"We've had a BOLO out for him, but no hits," Bogie said, "which is why this case went cold."

"Now it's hot again," Mac said.

Chapter Three

SCI Greene, Maximum Security Prison
Waynesburg, Pennsylvania

Joshua Thornton hated pat downs.

While he was aware that some of the most violent men in the state were locked up on the other side of the security gate through which he was passing, Joshua felt violated when the guard ran his thick palms up and down his body in search of anything that could be used as a weapon.

"Joshua…" The slightly built, blond haired man waiting on the other side of the entrance greeted him with a hug and a slap on the back. "Thank you so much for coming. I knew I could count on you."

"Only because you asked, Reverend Brody." Joshua clasped his hand into both of his. "If it was anybody else …" He slipped his watch back on his wrist, and put his wallet and cell phone in the inside breast pocket of his sports coat. "Like I told you, my contract with Hancock County forbids me from taking on private clients—"

"This isn't about handling Oliver Cartwright's appeal. He's not looking for his conviction and sentence to be overturned. He'd confessed to killing those women and he's made his peace with God." Reverend Body gestured at the cold block walls. "You'd be surprised how many people turn to God when they end up here. For many, it's only by the grace of God that some of them are able to survive."

"I'm a small town prosecutor. What can I possibly do for a monster like Oliver Cartwright?" Out of respect for the church reverend, Joshua refrained from spitting out the name of the man who had confessed to abducting, raping, and killing six women during a murder spree the decade before.

"He *was* a monster." Reverend Brody escorted him down the corridor to where they were to meet with the prisoner. "He's also a man and still is."

"Tell that to the families of his victims," Joshua told him. "I'm sorry. Have you forgotten that I'm the father of two girls who are now around the age of his victims?"

"I totally understand," the pastor replied. "Cartwright truly appreciates you coming to see him. We don't have much time. They're only allowing us fifteen minutes." He led Joshua down a barren concrete hallway and past a series of metal doors until they reached one with two guards standing outside.

"This is Joshua Thornton," Reverend Brody said to one of the guards. "He's on the visitor list."

One of the guards checked his clipboard before nodding to his partner to unlock the door and Reverend Brody led him into the visitor's room.

Joshua regretted his grandmother teaching him to have the utmost respect for those people of authority, especially the clergy. To deny a request made by a reverend or priest was like saying no to God—something you never want to do.

What could a serial killer not fighting for an appeal of his conviction possibly want from me? What's listening to Grandmomma getting me into now?

From what Joshua had learned about Oliver Cartwright, that was the one thing the two men had in common. They had both been raised by their grandmothers, who were strong-willed women. Firm on discipline. Long on love.

How, but for the grace of God, did I ended up where I am and Oliver Cartwright grow up to become a monster? How is it that I grew up to have a distinguished career with five good kids; while this man has been locked up for the rest of his living days for killing seven women? Was it the reason behind why his own parents didn't raise him?

Joshua's parents had been killed in a car accident while driving back home from a second honeymoon.

Oliver Cartwright's father was unknown. His mother had run off to Hollywood to be a star, and had ended up a prostitute on Hollywood and Vine.

Joshua was startled out of his thoughts by the clearing of a throat. The reverend was waiting for him to join them at the table on the other side of the room.

The clang of the door shutting behind him made him jump.

The serial killer had his head bowed with his palms pressed together. Reverend Brody placed his hand on his shoulder to join him in prayer. Joshua remained on the other side of the room until they were finished.

The man in the orange overalls lifted his head and smiled so broadly at Joshua that his shiny scalp wrinkled around his ears. "Mr. Joshua Thornton. You did come." He turned to the pastor. "It really works. Prayers are answered. I can't believe he came." He turned back to the lawyer. "I prayed you would come."

The absence of words caused Joshua to answer with a silent nod. He wondered if this was some sort of mistake.

The serial killer that had held Pittsburgh and its surrounding area in a grip of terror during the summer of 2003 was a devil-worshipper with a full head of blond hair and bushy beard.

Is it really possible for a serial killing atheist to become a born again Christian? Has to be a trick.

"Sit down, Joshua." Reverend Brody offered him a chair at the table.

"Thank you for your prayers, Reverend." Oliver clasped his hand. "They're helping. I've been sleeping better, and now Joshua Thornton is here—"

"I'm not making any promises," Joshua sat in the chair across from him. "The reverend didn't even tell me what this was about. I only came because he asked."

"But now you're here." Oliver flashed a wide grin filled with yellow teeth. "I have faith that you'll help, and God will make things right. He is just. That's why I'm here." He indicated the prison walls. "*This* is where I belong."

Joshua slowly nodded his head before casting him a sidelong glance.

The killer's smile dropped. "I know what you're thinking. I'm a monster. Right? That's what you're thinking."

Joshua couldn't stop the glare that he flashed across the table at the killer.

"You're right. I was a monster." Oliver let out an evil-sounding laugh. "I confessed. Hell, I was proud of what I did. Now, I'm ashamed of it. I'm ashamed of what I was. I pray for those women—and their families." The grin dropped from his face. "It took about seven years to sink in, but God did it. Suddenly, it all happened and—I'm not the same man I was when I killed those women. That man is dead."

"You were born again?" Joshua was still suspicious.

"I've asked for forgiveness—why He would forgive me? Anyone would forgive me?—but—" Oliver choked up. "I know I don't deserve it. That's why, I want there to be one good thing that I leave behind." Tears came to his eyes. "That's why you're here. I can't do it, but you can. Reverend Body said you're the one man who cares enough to do it—not for me—for her."

"Her who?" Joshua asked.

"Jane Doe," Oliver said. "Victim Number Four."

"He wasn't charged for her murder," Reverend Brody said.

"Because I didn't do her."

"That's why you weren't charged with her murder," Joshua said. "You were charged with six murders out of seven victims attributed to you."

"That's right," Oliver said, "Everyone thinks I did that fourth victim. I hear about it. The news says I killed seven women, but I didn't do Jane Doe. Since they all think I did her, no one is trying to find out who did. No one even knows who she is. She has people out there, Mr. Thornton. Maybe they know what happened to her. Maybe they don't. But there's one thing I do know. Someone killed her and it wasn't me; and she deserves justice just like those women I did kill."

He reached out to touch Joshua's hand. During the long drive from Chester, West Virginia, to the prison, Joshua couldn't fathom how he could sit in the same room with this man. Now, he was touching his hand. Joshua could feel the sincerity in the warmth of his dry scaly fingers.

"I want one good thing to come out of my being on this Earth. Make it this. Don't do it for me. I don't deserve it. But Jane Doe does. Do it for her."

Looking down at the killer's hand on his, Joshua tried to recall what he had heard about Jane Doe.

Victim Number Four.

The police working the case didn't release much about her murder. A county prosecuting attorney in Hancock County, West Virginia, Joshua wasn't involved in the investigation. All he knew was what the media reported.

Like the other victims, her body was found naked in a field.

Oliver Cartwright had forced his victims into their cars and then drove them to a vacant field where he'd raped and strangled them. Leaving his victims naked where he killed them, Cartwright would return the victim's car to the shopping center from which he had snatched them, and leave their clothes neatly folded on the driver's seat.

Jane Doe was never identified. No one knew where she had come from or how she had ended up murdered in a field.

Oliver squeezed Joshua's hand while gazing at him with tears in his eyes. "Help Jane, Mr. Thornton. Please."

The door opened to the cell. "Sorry, gentlemen. Time's up."

Joshua turned to Cartwright. "I will. I promise. I'll do everything I can to make things right for Jane Doe. I'll do it for both of you."

 C3 ഉ C8 ഉ

What a way to start a vacation.

For the first time in Joshua's forty-five years, he was home alone. All of his five children were gone and he had the whole house on the corner of Rock Spring Boulevard in Chester, West Virginia, to himself.

Home alone was a big thing. Joshua had gone from his grandmother's home to the Naval Academy, where he had lived in a dorm. From the Naval Academy, he had gotten married and lived with his wife, Valerie. They immediately began a family with their first born being twins. Valerie's sudden death had left him with five children, most of them teenagers.

Now, they were leaving the nest one by one. This summer seemed like one long graduation with one son, Murphy, graduating from the Naval Academy and moving to Washington to begin his first assignment at the Pentagon. Daughter Sarah graduated from Oak Glen High School and was taking her brother's place at the Naval Academy. Her summer consisted of plebe training in Annapolis.

The week after Sarah's graduation, Joshua Junior, Murphy's twin, graduated with a bachelor in pre-law from Pennsylvania State University. After a summer of teaching as an associate professor, he would be starting law school in August.

Daughter Tracy was thrilled to receive a highly coveted summer internship position at the Ritz Carlton in New York City. She was now learning top culinary secrets from some of the world's most respected chefs.

They grow up fast. The last Thornton left in the nest was sixteen-year-old Donny, who was spending the month at the Outer Banks with his aunt and uncle and their children.

While waiting for those pangs of empty nest to hit, Joshua planned for a two-week vacation from his job as Hancock County's prosecuting attorney to fly solo and enjoy every minute.

After waving goodbye to Donny when he rode off with Sarah to head east; Joshua went inside, stripped off his clothes, and went room to room naked. Then, he ordered a take-out pizza, drank soda straight from the liter bottle, and put it back in the fridge without the cap.

When he woke up that first morning, Joshua thought about Reverend Brody's request for him to visit Oliver Cartwright in prison. He hemmed-and-hawed before finally agreeing at the last minute to go. He'd feel guilty if he didn't.

Joshua wasn't going to embark on this investigation so much for Oliver Cartwright as he was for Jane Doe's family. He couldn't imagine what it would be like if Jane Doe was one of his two daughters, and he didn't know what had happened to her.

Modern technology had become a Godsend. While drinking a cup of coffee at Starbucks, Joshua searched the Internet on his smart phone to find the names of the lead investigating officers in the Oliver Cartwright murders. Lieutenant Hank Gregory, the lead officer, had died. The second lead investigator, Detective Cameron Gates was stationed at the state police barracks in Gibsonia, Pennsylvania, off Interstate 79.

Within two hours of leaving Waynesburg, Joshua pulled his SUV into the police barracks, in hopes of having a sit down with the homicide detective. At least, that was his hope.

As expected, the state police barracks was more spacious and contained most of the coveted conveniences of modern technology. It was a big step up from Hancock County's small Sheriff Department.

After being directed to the homicide section, Joshua was greeted by an obese woman with dark shaggy hair and bangs that fell into her black eyes. On her way out, she made a U-turn on the other side of the door to follow him into the squad room. "May I help you?"

"I'm here to see Detective Cameron Gates," Joshua answered her.

"Who's asking?" Licking her lips, she looked him up and down.

Behind her, Joshua saw another woman watching him from behind her desk. Her short wavy audburn hair and tan jacket gave her a casual youthful appearance. She flashed him a wide grin that pushed her laugh lines up to frame her greenish-brown eyes. For most women, the wrinkles that come with age would be considered unattractive. Hers served to accentuate her high cheekbones.

Her grin was welcoming, while that of the short woman blocking his path resembled the sneer of a predator spotting her next conquest. Tapping the end of a cigarette on a black leather case, she undressed the man with silver wavy hair with her eyes.

He handed her his business card, which she read out loud. "Joshua Thornton, County Prosecuting Attorney, Hancock County, West Virginia." Her big, grating, voice drew the unwanted attention of anyone who had not noticed them before. "So, Joshua Thornton, what brings you here from West-By-God-Virginia?" Laughing at what he did not know, she turned around for applause from the others in the squad room.

Judging by the amusement of everyone, except the pretty woman, the fat cigarette smoker was someone of authority.

"The Oliver Cartwright case," he told her without humor.

The laughter stopped.

The grin fell from the smoker's round face. "Are you his attorney?"

"No," Joshua replied. "I'm here to ask questions about the victim he wasn't charged for killing. Jane Doe. Victim Number Four."

The pretty woman was now sitting up tall in her seat.

"You've come to the wrong place, Joshua Thornton," the smoker said.

"This precinct has the lead on Jane Doe's case. It's never been closed."

"Unofficially, it's closed," she argued. "Everyone knows Oliver Cartwright killed her."

"If he killed her why wasn't her murder brought up at his trial?" he countered. "Was it because you had evidence to prove he didn't kill her? Evidence that could lead to identifying her and finding her real killer? That's why the prosecutors steered clear of even mentioning her to the jury. If they had, the defense would have been able to make a case for reasonable doubt."

"There was no doubt," the smoker yelled. "He was tried and convicted. He confessed."

"Not to killing Jane Doe!" Joshua felt conviction that hadn't been there before for finding out the truth about Jane Doe's murder. Any uncertainty he had felt before about the killer's innocence in this murder was now gone. "That's why I'm here."

She laughed. "To help a serial rapist and killer?"

Grins came to the faces of those around her, but not on the face of the pretty woman. Her mouth was tight. Joshua sensed that her heart was pumping as hard as his.

"No, to help a murder victim."

"Well, you're not getting it here." She ripped his business card in half and tossed it in the direction of a trash can. "I know your game. You prove Cartwright didn't kill Jane Doe, and then you make a case that he was wrongly convicted; and, the next thing you know, he's out. I won't have any part in it."

"Cartwright was never charged with killing Jane Doe," Joshua argued. "Finding out who killed her won't have any bearing on getting him out, which he won't since he's not seeking an appeal."

"Get out of here!"

Any possible unwanted attraction the fat smoker may have had for him when he first walked in was now gone. Her eyes glaring, she rushed to close up the small bit of space between them, thrust her double chin at him, and pointed a flabby arm towards the door.

As ugly as Joshua had found her before, she was even more so up close. The glares he saw on the rest of the faces in the squad room indicated that there was no hope for any of them coming to his defense. Even the pretty woman was no longer at her desk.

With a shake of his head, Joshua left.

ℭ   ℬ   ℭ   ℬ

Joshua's cell phone was vibrating on his hip before he reached the car.

"Have you had lunch yet, Joshua Thornton?" Her tone was much more pleasant than that of the fat smoker.

The question reminded him that he had left for the prison early that morning with nothing more than a pot of coffee. His stomach rumbled. "What do you have in mind?"

"I'm only going to say this once," she said in a low voice like a kidnapper relaying a ransom pick up. "Pull out of the barracks and turn right. Take the William Flynn Highway for ten-point-two miles. When you come to the fork, stay to the left. Stay on the Pennsylvania 28 South to Pittsburgh. Keep right at the fork and merge onto 279 South and then take Interstate 376 West. Take exit 68 at Parkway Center Drive. There's a burger joint off on the left. They have a drive-thru. Get me a double cheeseburger with lettuce, tomato, and only a swipe of mayo. Only a swipe. If I so much as see a drop of mayo, we're through. I want you to also order a large waffle fries with seasoned salt, a chocolate milkshake, and a small skim milk. It has to be fat-free. Milk with fat gives Irving gas. Oh, and don't forget the straw and napkins."

Joshua was smiling. "Light on the mayo. Waffle fries with seasoned salt. Chocolate milkshake. Fat-free milk. Fat gives Irving gas.—Who's Irving?"

"My partner," she answered. "Feel free to get something for yourself. You're buying. When you come out of the burger joint, turn right and get on Greentree Road. When you come to a fork, bare to the right onto Ridgemont Drive.—"

"Is this a joke?" Joshua yanked open the door to the glove compartment for a pen and paper.

"No," she replied. "When you come to Springfield Street turn right. Take the first left onto New York Street and follow that all the way to a dead end. You'll end at a hay field with clover. You'll know you're at the right place when you see an abandoned barn with a Mail Pouch sign painted on the side … unless it's blown down since the murder, in which case you won't see it, and will have to assume you're at the right spot. Meet me there in forty-five minutes. Don't be late."

"What if I am?"

"I'll faint from hunger and you'll need to give me mouth-to-mouth to revive me." She was still laughing when she hung up the phone.

Joshua stared at the phone in his hand. She reminded him of someone. Both her laugh and the warm feeling he got in his heart when he heard it. It was an eerily familiar feeling that made him wonder if he knew her from someplace.

When he hung up, he thought of how pretty she looked sitting behind the desk. *Oh, how sweet it would be to give her mouth-to-mouth rescusitation.* Turning the key to start the engine in his car, he almost hoped she would be unconscious from hunger when he met her.

ଔ   ଟ   ଓ   ଚ

It wasn't until Joshua was waiting for their burgers and fries at the drive thru that the thought crossed his mind, *Suppose the caller wasn't the pretty woman? Suppose she turns out to be some lunatic even uglier than the fat smoker?*

Checking the time on the dashboard of his SUV, Joshua saw that he would have to wait another fifteen minutes to find out if his assumption was right.

When you assume, you make an ass of you and me.

The food smelled too good for a hungry man to resist. While watching for the street signs on the busy freeway, Joshua resisted the urge to reach inside the bag to chow down on the waffle fries.

He worked his way through the streets on the outskirts of Pittsburgh, where the landscape changed from high rises and office complexes to rural farmland waiting to be developed.

The broken down barn popped into view at the dead end of a subdivision road, which abruptly changed from paved to dirt without warning. Joshua didn't notice the end of the road until his SUV dropped off the end of the pavement with a jolt that sent the food flying off the seat. It was only due to his quick reflexes that he caught the bag in mid-air with one hand.

A white SUV was parked in the field. The pretty woman in the tan jacket was waiting on the tailgate. He saw that her lower half, clad in black slacks, was as pretty as the top.

Thank you, God! She looks even better outside the police station.

When Joshua pulled up to park behind her car, he saw that her attention was divided between him and something next to her on the tailgate. At first, he thought it was a doll or stuffed animal that she was stroking.

Then, when he pulled his SUV up closer, it rolled over to let her scratch his tummy. It was a live animal with long black fur ... and a white stripe ... down the length of its back. *Is that a skunk she's petting?*

"Did you bring my bribe?" she called out when he climbed out of his car. She jumped down from the tailgate.

"Is that what this is?" He handed the bag to her before reaching back into the car for the shakes.

The animal paced back and forth on the tailgate.

As if she might be unaware of what she had been petting, Joshua asked her in a low voice, "Is that a skunk?"

"No." She dug into the bag for the milk. "That's Irving. He's a Maine Coon. He only looks like a skunk."

"That's a cat?" Carrying the shakes, Joshua went up to the tailgate for a closer look.

Irving was much larger than a skunk. With his long silky black and white coat, which had the identical markings of a skunk, and white tufts that shot out of his black ears, he could be easily mistaken for the odious forest creature.

Seeing food coming his way, Irving rose up on his hind legs to inspect the milkshakes. His mistress took a blue plastic dish from the back of the SUV and placed it on the ground. With a meow, he forgot about the shakes and jumped down to await the milk that was to serve as his lunch.

Joshua noticed a leash, cat harness, pet bed, and assorted cat toys in the back of the SUV. "Do you take him to work with you?"

"When you're the department's top homicide detective, they make some allowances." She stroked the cat before standing up to dive into the bag for her lunch. "You didn't notice him curled up in his bed under my desk, did you?" She laughed while dividing the food between them. "You should see the reaction we get from suspects and witnesses who're under the influence."

"I can imagine." He took the burger she offered him.

"I'll spill my guts while we eat."

They sat on the tail gate with the food between them. Judging by how she dove into the double cheeseburger, she wasn't joking about being hungry. He waited for her to wash down her first bite of the burger with the milk shake before pointing out that she had not given him her name.

"Haven't you guessed?" she replied with a sly grin that brought dimples to her cheeks. "Detective Cameron Gates. I was the second lead detective investigating the Cartwright murders." She shook his hand with greasy long fingers. "I'm the one you came in to see."

"Who was the obnoxious woman that wouldn't let me see you?" Since she was meeting with him on the sly, Joshua didn't think she was a comrade of the fat smoker.

"My boss," Cameron said. "Lieutenant Sherry Bixby. She wasn't on the team during the investigation. She's made some bad political moves and ticked the wrong people off. She's got too many miles under her belt for the brass to fire her, so they were just looking for someplace to put her until she gets in her time to retire. That's how we got stuck with her."

Joshua pieced Bixby's reluctance together. "If a murder attributed to Cartwright proves to be someone else on her watch, then her career is over."

"It's already over," she said. "People have told me that she's a drunk. She claims to go out to her car for a smoke every hour. She does insist on having a cocktail hour, but then I know a lot of cops that stop for a drink after shift. It's more with Bixby, though. She has wild mood swings and she doesn't think straight. She makes bad decisions. That's why she's not out in the field."

"What if she knew you were meeting with me to discuss the Cartwright case after she tossed me out?" Joshua asked between bites of his burger.

"What if?" she replied. "I've never cared about making friends and influencing people. I became a detective because I care about the victim who can't ask for help. I'm not into making friends. Irving's the first partner I ever had that worked out. Yeah, we fight and fuss; but Irving's never asked to be reassigned to the bomb squad to get away from me."

Unsure if she was serious or not, Joshua cocked his head at her. "Has that happened?"

"Do you really want to know the answer to that question?"

"No." The reference to the skunk cat made Joshua smile. "If Irving is like most cats I know, he's happy as long as you leave him alone."

"And I'm happy as long as he leaves me alone."

"Then why do you take him to work with you?"

Clearing her throat, she glanced down as if to ensure Irving wasn't listening. He was still lapping up his lunch. She told Joshua in a low voice, "Irving has issues."

"Who doesn't?" he whispered back.

Smiling, she shook a fry in his direction while saying, "I like you."

Holding up his shake to take a long sip, he asked "Tell me about your issues."

"I'm pugnacious when I'm on a case. That's one word that has been used to describe me. Another supervisor said I'm like a dog with a bone...I don't know when to let go. That's why I wasn't picked to head the division even though Gregory recommended me for it after I helped him catch Cartwright." She took a long drink of her shake. "Those are my issues. Want to tell me yours?" She ate another fry.

"No." He watched her chew the fry she popped into her mouth before taking another bite of the burger. There was something familiar about her.

Seeming to sense him studying her, she looked down at the burger in her hand while wiping away a stray lock of hair that dipped into her eyes. The tan of her jacket brought out the green specks in her brown eyes, which were framed by minute laugh lines that added character to her face. With her shaggy, cinnamon-colored hair that fell to the collar of her jacket, Cameron looked like a girl. In her profession, calling her a girl was a slam. She didn't look strong enough to handle herself when the situation called for it.

He told her, "You knew before I came into that station that Cartwright didn't kill Jane Doe."

"Gregory and I never said he did it. It was the media that assumed he did it because of the similarity between this murder and those he'd committed."

They paused to take long sips of their milkshakes.

"Any idea about who she is?" he asked. "Do you have any suspects for her murder?"

"No, but I know someone who does know."

"Who?"

"The Ghost."

Digesting what she had said, Joshua was staring at her with his mouth hanging open when she turned to look at him. Her gaze was soft on him. The corner of her lips curled. When she reached out to him, his reflexes made him fall back quicker than he really wanted.

"You have mayo on your cheek." She wiped his cheek with two fingers, which she kept on his cheek longer than necessary, while locking her eyes on his. When she leaned in to kiss him, he didn't know which surprised him more: Her kissing him, or him letting her?

It hit him—He realized who she reminded him of. It was in her kiss. Valerie. His late wife. The touch of her lips. The warm feeling that raced from the pit of his stomach and up to his chest to quicken the beat of his heart.

His tone was low when he found his voice. "You move fast."

Her eyes were still locked on his. "I've learned something in this job. Life is short. When you see a good thing, go for it. You may not live to get a second chance."

The corner of her lips curled. "Irving likes you, too. That means a lot. Most men run away while screaming like little girls when they see him."

Having completed his lunch, Irving was sitting on Joshua's foot to give himself a bath. Meticulously, he licked his paws before wiping his face with them.

Sensing that the moment was getting hotter than he wanted, Joshua cleared his throat and turned his attention to their empty wrappers and bag. He rolled up the wrappers to put into the sack. "Who's the Ghost? Are we talking about Jane Doe's ghost?"

"Maybe." She was still drinking her milkshake when she hopped down from the tailgate and turned around to reach into a worn leather briefcase tucked in alongside of the rear compartment. "I never met her. She started calling me before and during Cartwright's trial. Of course, the media dredged up everything about the murders, and Jane Doe's picture was splashed all over the television and Internet, asking for anyone who knew who she was to call us. Low and behold, I get a call from a woman asking *me* questions about the Jane Doe case."

Joshua asked, "What did you tell her?"

"I've been at this for a while," Cameron said. "I only told her what was for public knowledge. The thought even crossed my mind that it was a trick by the defense lawyers, but like you said, Cartwright was never charged with Jane Doe's murder."

"Did the informant tell you who Jane was?"

Shaking her head, Cameron pulled her briefcase forward and dug through it. "I got no names. Not for Jane or the informant. When I pressed her for something to call her, she said she was the ghost of Jane Doe. That's why I call her the Ghost." She slapped his thigh with a notepad. "Here are my notes for the case. My conversations with the Ghost are in the back."

Joshua flipped through the pages to make his way to the end of the notepad. Cameron was organized. She had dates and times for everything.

"The Ghost had a thick accent," she recalled. "She knew Jane Doe was a natural redhead. One would have assumed she had a dye job. She also asked if Jane Doe had an appendectomy scar. That wasn't released to the media. Only someone who knew her would have known that."

"Then the Ghost did know who Jane Doe was," Joshua said. "Did she tell you anything else?"

Cameron shook her head. "It was very frustrating. From that point on, she was asking me questions, which I couldn't answer because it was an open case. I couldn't get anything from her. I tried to get her to come in. She said she couldn't. I sense she was scared. I explained that if she wanted us to find out who killed her friend or whatever—"

"Did she think Oliver Cartwright did it?" Joshua interrupted to ask.

"No," Cameron said. "She knew from the get-go that he didn't do it. She told me he didn't do it. I think the killer was someone the victim knew. That's why the Ghost kept asking me questions. She was trying to figure it out on her own. Thing is, she didn't give me anything to help us. She started calling me out of the blue, and out of the blue, she stopped calling."

Joshua noted the date of the last call.

Thursday, September 2, 2004. 4:30 pm. Ghost asks if forensics answered her question about murder weapon possibly being a piano wire. Answer that it could have been. Ask Ghost if she knows of someone who could have done it with such a weapon. No answer. Repeat request for Ghost to come in to tell us what she knows to help catch Jane Doe's killer. Ghost says she'll take care of it. Hangs up.

Cameron pressed her finger against the last entry. "Never heard from her again."

"I wonder if she did take care of it."

"Your guess is as good as mine." She pulled a case file out of the briefcase and handed it to him. "My bootleg copy of the Jane

Doe murder case. We're going to be needing this if we're going to find out who really killed her."

He took the file and thumbed through the reports. "Is this the royal 'we'?"

"Of course." She backed up from him. "Gregory is dead. Bixby won't allow anyone in the department to work on it. You certainly don't expect me and Irving to do this all on our own, do you?" She let out a loud sarcastic laugh. "I'm just a girl."

She batted her eyelashes at him and whirled around. Her jacket lifted to reveal her police shield and gun clipped to her belt.

Joshua joined in her laughter. He had that warm familiar feeling again and liked it.

Now this is the way to spend a vacation—solving a murder with a stunning woman...and a skunk cat name Irving. What would my kids say if they knew?

Finished with his bath, Irving jumped up onto the tailgate. As if to thank Joshua for bringing his lunch, he rubbed the whole length of his long body against his arm from nose to tail and then back again.

"Picture this." Cameron came back up to where Joshua was sitting on her tail gate. "Jane Doe's murder was crying out copycat, but we had three other unsolved murders, and then Cartwright killed his next victim. Our top priority back then was to get Cartwright off the streets. All of our man power was focused on catching the serial killer, not the copycat. By the time we nailed Cartwright, everyone had virtually forgotten about Jane Doe, and we didn't get any heat from the media, who assumed and lumped her murder in with those of his victims."

"Meanwhile, Jane Doe's killer goes free." Joshua stood up from the tailgate.

Irving jumped down and trotted over to his mistress.

"Exactly." She closed the tail gate.

He looked down at the thick folder in his hand. "Tell me what you do know about Jane Doe. She had an appendectomy."

She led him over to the edge of the field. While she was speaking, they waded through the clover and tall grass. "A farmer found her body on June 10, 2003. He saw buzzards overhead and thought it was a dead deer." She stopped to point down to her feet. "He found her right here."

The growth of tall grass in fertile soil left no tell-tale sign that it was the spot where death had rested almost ten years before.

Cameron continued, "Good thing he checked. He was out here to mow the hay. If he hadn't …" With a shiver, she stared off across the field filled with clover swaying in the breeze. "She'd been dead over twenty-four hours."

Joshua studied the crime scene picture of her body that was clipped to the top of the reports in the file. Her wavy red hair was fanned out behind her where she had been sprawled out naked in the bed of clover. Having grown up with family in the farming business, he recalled that farm animals love the sweet taste of clover.

The bruise across her neck was dark against her gray flesh. "She was garroted," he said. "Cartwright strangled his victims from the front with his bare hands."

Cameron nodded her head. "That was the deal breaker for trying to charge Cartwright with the murder."

"Are there any signs of sexual assault?" He flipped through the coroner's report to find the official statement.

"She had sexual intercourse shortly before she was killed, but not directly before. The ME said it was most likely consensual."

Flipping through the report, Joshua led her back to the road where Irving sat waiting. "He collected semen from her body."

"The sample wasn't viable for DNA analysis."

Joshua asked her, "Did you ever find any leads, besides the Ghost, in identifying her?"

"At the time of the murder, her picture was all over the news for more than a week," Cameron said. "We never located her car. Cartwright would always drive the car back to the shopping center from where he'd snatched his victim."

"Forget about Cartwright," he said. "We're looking for someone else. How about her fingerprints?"

"We ran her fingerprints through AFIS and there were no hits," she said.

"Okay." Joshua studied Jane Doe's picture and the ME's report. "No body piercings or tattoos. There's some alcohol in her blood, but nothing significant. Appendectomy scar. Her lungs were clear. She wasn't a smoker. Mid-to late twenties."

"Cartwright's victims were late teens to early twenties."

"My point is this woman is not malnourished. No drugs, no—She was well taken care of. Someone cared about her."

"The Ghost," Cameron said. "But, according to her, she was taking care of it."

Joshua was reading another line in the autopsy report. "X-rays show the victim had extensive dental work possibly originating in Europe, most likely Britain." He turned to her. "Did you know that the most expensive dental work in the world is done in Britain?"

"I did not know that," Cameron replied. "She may be European." She slapped her forehead with her open palm. "The Ghost spoke with a European accent. Of course!"

She looked up in time to see a jet ascending overhead as it took off from the airport located several exits up the freeway. "The airport isn't far from here. The killer could have snatched her from there shortly after she arrived from someplace else. She's not local. That's why no one recognized her picture on the news. Her body was dumped. That was another thing. The body showed signs of lividity and there were carpet fibers in her hair." She showed him the place in the forensics report where it reported the carpet fibers.

"Can you run her fingerprints again?" Joshua asked. "This time run them through the international database. If she's a foreigner, you may get a hit. Someone somewhere in this world has to know this woman."

She laughed. "I'll get into so much trouble if I go into evidence and ask them to run her fingerprints through the international database. Do you have any idea how embarrassing it would be for Bixby if we found Jane Doe's real killer on her watch?"

"I don't want you to get into trouble on my account." He closed the folder and handed it back to her.

She hugged the case file to her chest. "I didn't say I wasn't going to do it, darling." She brushed her fingers across his cheek while gazing into his blue eyes. "I just said I was going to have lots of fun doing it."

Chapter Four

Mac tried to ignore Gnarly.

After more than a year of living with the beast, Mac held on to a sliver of hope that if he ignored the cold snout poking him on the cheek and neck that Gnarly would give up and return to his den under the bed.

Another two hours of sleep wasn't going to happen. Not as long as there were ducks invading Gnarly's territory on the dock or squirrels gathering nuts in his yard. When Mac didn't respond to the poking, Gnarly resorted to a full body assault by jumping up onto the bed and digging him out from under the bedding.

Cursing, Mac threw off the covers and looked over at the other side of the king-sized bed.

It was empty—as it was every morning. The pillow and sheets showed the usual signs of having been slept in. The bedding on "her side" even contained a hint of Archie's scent.

Mac paused to appreciate the sweetness of the smell, until Gnarly tagged him in the back with his front paws with such force that he landed face down onto her pillow.

"Okay, I'm coming." Mac shoved his arms through the sleeves of his bathrobe on his way down the stairs. He tied the belt tight around his waist before yanking the back door open to let Gnarly out onto the deck.

The German Shepherd's barks resembled a morning wakeup call when he charged off the deck to the dock where a flock of ducks waited to be chased out into the lake.

The granite floor sent a cold shock from the bottom of Mac's bare feet and up through his shoulders. Trying to avoid the freezing touch, he tiptoed into the kitchen to hit the switch to start the coffee brewing. While waiting for his first dose of caffeine, he peered out the kitchen window and marveled at the turn of events.

Whoever would have guessed an underpaid cop would end up like this?

The first sunrays of the day caused a mist to rise from the lake to create an eerie effect. Shivering, Mac pulled the bathrobe tight around his bare shoulders and chest.

Through chattering teeth, he smiled at Gnarly barking at the ducks from the end of the dock. They swam out to the end of the cove before turning around and quacking back at him. Their quacks sounded as if they were taunting him to come get them. When Gnarly felt particularly feisty, which he often was, he would.

Go get 'em, Gnarly.

Three beeps signaled that his coffee had finished brewing. Mac tiptoed over to the counter to fill his mug. With the sun not quite up yet, it was still too cold to enjoy his coffee on the deck. So he stretched out on the sofa to wake up while enjoying a different view.

Ilysa Ramsay's last painting. Her lost work of art.

Propped up against the wall, it filled the space on the far side of his living room.

Mac stared at the redhead in the emerald gown.

Ilysa Ramsey was a beautiful woman indeed. She was also talented. How ironic that, before her death, she chose to surround herself, in this painting, with those most suspected of killing her. Was she predicting her own death?

Ilysa's blue eyes seemed to jump out of the painting at him. Mac jumped. It was as if the painting had come to life.

Must have gone back to sleep.

"I see Gnarly has cleared the perimeter." Archie's voice woke him up the rest to of the way. "We can feel safe again. Coffee brewed?" She went into the kitchen to get the answer for herself and feed Gnarly.

His first chore of the day completed, Gnarly was ready for the next items on his list: breakfast. First, he had an appetizer in the form of a biscuit, to be followed by his breakfast. He didn't care who served them to him, as long as someone did so in a timely fashion.

Mac sat up and returned to staring at the painting.

What's wrong with this painting? It's something to do with her eyes. The expression. Like Ilysa is pleading for me to find her killer.

The ruby jewels around her neck resembled drops of blood. Her blood spilled during her murder—committed *after* she had done this painting.

But Ilysa's throat wasn't slashed. She was bludgeoned to death with a hammer. So she didn't predict her own murder.

"Why don't you go back to bed?" Archie startled him out of his thoughts when she slipped onto the sofa next to him. She had on the same rose-colored bathrobe she had worn the night before.

Mac remembered his pleasure when she had slipped it off the night before, and how she had consumed him, as she always did ... afterwhich, she slipped away in the middle of the night to return to her cottage.

"I got lonely," he said in a tone devoid of any signs of pouting.

"Do you want me to keep you company?" she asked in a playful tone.

"That's a very tempting offer, but Bogie and David are coming by. They're taking me to go look at the Ramsay crime scene."

"Then you're being invited onto the case. That's good."

With pride in his voice, Mac told her, "David is taking me on as a contractor."

"Contractor?"

"Only for this case," he said. "He can do that since I'm certified for law enforcement. I may be retired, but my state credentials are up to date. Who knows? Maybe I'll decide I'm not cut out to be a rich retired millionaire."

She slipped her hand into his robe to brush her fingers across his chest. "When are they coming?"

"A couple of hours." He didn't object when she slid over to press her body to his.

"Do you want to go back to bed?"

"Maybe." He was coy. "You know, you're allowed to stay the night with me. You don't have to keep slipping out in the middle of the night like some vampire that needs to get back to her coffin before sunrise."

"I know." Taking his hand, she led him to the stairs.

"Then why do you?"

"Because I'm more comfortable in my own bed."

"I'll come sleep over there."

On the stairs, she whirled around. "And leave Gnarly here by himself?"

"I'll bring him with me. He can chaperone."

"Yeah, I can see he'll make a great chaperone," she noted with sarcasm while pointing out that Gnarly was already stretched out on the sofa that they had just vacated.

☙ ❧ ☙ ❧

"I think about that day every time I drive past this place," Bogie told Mac and David when they stepped out of his cruiser at the Hathaway estate.

With most of its citizens listed in *Who's Who*, Spencer was considered uptown from nearby McHenry and Oakland. Pelican Court's sole resident was a step above that. The sprawling mansion, tennis courts, pool, and gardens made Spencer Manor look like a child's back yard playhouse.

With a somber expression that made his bushy mustache press up his nostrils, Bogie peered up at the studio where Ilysa Ramsay was murdered.

Mac followed his gaze to the building looking out over the lake. "That's not a guest house," Bogie said. "It's a five-car underground garage. Ramsay's art studio was upstairs. She had a kitchenette and bedroom in the loft. She practically lived up there when she was painting, which was that whole summer."

David added, "Neal Hathaway found her body."

Bogie told Mac, "Hathaway states that she had slipped out of bed during the night to go to the studio to paint. That was not unusual. When she'd get tired, she would go to bed up in the loft. Hathaway got up that morning and went looking for her. That was when he found her."

"May I help you?" the maid called out to them from the front door.

"Good morning, Greta," Bogie strode up to the porch. "I don't know if you remember me. I'm Deputy Chief Art Bogart."

"I remember you." She looked each of them up and down. When she came to Mac's unfamiliar face, she kept her gaze on him.

When he had been a homicide detective, Mac discovered that housekeeping staff made invaluable witnesses. Good domestic employees make a point of being practically invisible while noticing everything. It's a necessity in order to meet their employers' every need without getting in the way.

When it came to criminal investigations, the problem was getting them to talk. They were often as loyal to their employers as they were observant.

Mac placed Greta's accent as being Swedish. It wasn't as easy to place her age. She was tall and slender to the point of being skinny. Like in the painting, her face was gaunt, which seemed accentuated by her long straight silver hair that fell to a blunt cut at her shoulders and bangs cut straight across.

David answered the question in her eyes. "This is Mac Faraday. He's working with our department as a special investigator on Ms. Ramsay's murder case. May we speak to Mr. Hathaway?"

"He's in a meeting." Like a guard, she didn't move from where she blocked their way through the door.

Mac replied, "We can wait until he's available to meet with us."

After casting a stern glance at each of them, she went to find her boss. Assuming she had left the door cracked open to serve as an invitation, Mac stepped inside.

He gaped in wonder at the white elegance of the foyer that stretched three floors up to the cathedral ceiling which contained two skylights. A crystal chandelier hanging down from the top peak of the ceiling to the second floor provided even more light to the bright white room.

On the left wall hung an oil painting, which provided a mirrored image of the curved staircase on the opposite side of the room. The only difference was that a silver haired man stood on the landing in the painting. He wore slacks, white shirt, and an open vest with his tie undone. He held a cigar in one hand and a drink in the other. His expression was one of supreme satisfaction. A brass plaque in the frame declared it to be a painting of Neal Hathaway.

Mac noted the signature in the lower corner of the painting: Ilysa Ramsay.

"David!" A call came from the top of the staircase. "Is that really you?" A younger version of the man in the painting trotted down the stairs. "How are you doing, bud?" He tucked the tennis racquet he was carrying under his arm and clasped David's hand into both of his. "Look at you. You look great."

"This is Scott," David said to Mac. "Neal Hathaway's son." He announced, "We've hired Mac to help us solve your step-mother's murder."

"Is he good?" Scott asked with a wink at David. "Should I be scared?"

"Only if you killed her. Mac's one of the best. Between him and Bogie, we've got the dream team of murder investigators on the case."

"All right!" He tapped his fist against David's before turning to Mac. "I met your police chief when I was learning self-defense in the Marine reserves." He let out a laugh. "I was awful."

Mac asked, "You were in the military?"

"We Hathaways are very America proud," Scott said. "I joined right out of college, got out, and then re-enlisted after September 11. David was my instructor for arm-to-arm combat training and about killed me."

"Scott was stationed in Europe when his stepmother was killed," David told Mac.

"I guess that means I'm not a suspect." Scott winked again. "But I could have hired someone to do it for me, I guess."

Mac replied without a grin. "That's correct."

Seeing that Mac was serious, Scott's smile fell.

An awkward silence filled the foyer before Scott said, "I'll take you to see Dad. I'm on my way to the club to meet a friend for tennis." He poked David in the chest with the racquet. "We need to arrange to get together. On the tennis court, I might be able to take you."

"I wouldn't bet on it," David said.

They were on their way through the house when Mac noticed what appeared to be a parlor. Spotting a grand piano, harp, and a lounging chair; he called out to the group about to step outside to the rear patio. "This is where the painting is set." David and Bogie followed him into the room.

"My mother was to be a musician," Scott told them. "The piano and harp were hers."

On a stand next to the harp rested another peculiar instrument that resembled a combination of a violin and ancient piano with a long series of keys attached to tangents along the frets. A bow rested next to it. Afraid of touching it for fear that it was of great monetary value, Mac asked Scott what it was.

"That's a nyckelharpa." Scott's grin betrayed his amusement. "You aren't the first to wonder about it. It's also known as a keyed fiddle. It's a Swedish instrument that dates back to 1300s. This one belongs to Greta. She taught my mom."

Mac asked, "Your mother passed away?"

"I was very young," Scott said while leading them back out toward the patio. "Susan plays the harp sometimes when we have parties. No one knows how to play that piano, but Dad keeps it because it was Mom's. He's sentimental like that."

Greta almost collided with all of them at the doors. "Mr. Hathaway can see you now. His meeting is breaking up."

Big in size and demeanor, Neal Hathaway seemed to cross the patio in two steps. Mac was pleased to see that, like him, Neal didn't feel obligated to wear his bank account. He was clad in khaki shorts and flip flops on his bare feet.

He clasped Mac's hand in both of his with a grip so strong that it threatened to break his fingers. When Neal shook his hand, it felt like he was going to pull Mac's arm from its socket. "I heard you were Robin Spencer's son. Is that right?"

"That's what the DNA tests say." Mac massaged his arm after their handshake.

"I loved your mother," Neal said. "Beauty and talent. You don't find that very often in a woman. My late wife was loaded with both."

Mac was able to place most of the group on the patio from the painting.

A woman sitting at the table rose to grasp Mac's hand. In contrast to their host, her slender hand was so limp and clammy that it reminded Mac of a dead fish. "Mr. Faraday, we have mutual friends. I'm Dr. Nancy Winter-Kaplan. This is my husband, Peyton Kaplan. He's Hathaway Industries vice president in charge of security."

Like in the painting, her black hair was mixed with silver strands cascading over her head like a spider web. Her lips and nails were bright red. Between the dark hair, blood red lips and nails, and pale complexion, she reminded Mac of a vampire.

When Nancy turned around to introduce her husband to Mac, they found him standing over a buxom blond writing notes on a wi-fi tablet at the table. The image of Peyton and Susan Dulin was strikingly similar to how Ilysa had painted them. His focus was directed down the front of her low-cut blouse to her abundant breasts.

"Peyton," his wife called sharply for his attention.

He almost knocked over a chair while snapping to attention.

"Mac Faraday is here," she said with a hiss in her voice. "Robin Spencer's son. He owns the Spencer Inn resort."

"Mac Faraday." Peyton clasped Mac's hand. "Great to finally meet you. I heard a lot about you."

There was a tinge of doubt in Mac's tone when he asked, "You're in charge of security at Hathaway Industries?" His instinct told him that he could trust Gnarly to guard his dinner plate more than this man.

"That would be me," Peyton told him. "Started out at the Pentagon over thirty years ago with the Army, went into intelligence, and now I'm in charge of some of the most sensitive information regarding defense satellites."

Neal slapped Peyton on the back. "It's not a job you hand off to someone you can't trust. I've known Peyton for over thirty years. We've been friends since college."

"You wouldn't believe the cutest shop that I found in McHenry." Laden down with shopping bags and packages, a woman in stiletto heels hurried out onto the patio. Overburdened, she barely made it to the table before spilling her treasures across papers that they had been working on.

"Rachel, did you leave anything in the store?" Scott asked.

"I didn't have time to try anything else on," Rachel said. "I had to come back to change before meeting some friends up at the inn for cocktails."

While Rachel went on to run down her social plans for that evening, David whispered to Mac, "Rachel Fields-Hathaway. Scott's wife."

She went on to show off her purchases. During the fashion show, she made a point of listing the cost of each item. The prices she rattled off made Mac, who had yet to adapt to his upper class bank account, physically ill. He could see by the set of Scott's jaw and the roll of Neal's eyes that they were equally disgusted by Rachel's talent for extravagance.

Like she was shooing a pest away, Nancy Kaplan gestured at the bags piled up in front of her. "Rachel, get your stuff out of here. Some people work for a living."

Scott's announcement reminded all of them of the police's presence. "David brought Mr. Faraday here to catch Ilysa's killer."

The police chief said, "We'd like to re-examine the crime scene."

"Why are you taking another look at her murder now?" Nancy asked.

"Because it's never been solved," Mac said.

Scott joined in. "I, for one, would like to see Ilysa's killer caught."

Neal said, "Bully! So would I!"

Nancy Kaplan squinted at Bogie. "What prompted all this renewed interest after eight years?" Her small dark eyes turned their attention to the police chief.

"We've had a break in the case," David said. "Mac Faraday has come into possession of Ilysa's last painting."

Silence fell over the patio like a blanket dropping out of the sky to land on top of them. Even Rachel seemed to forget about her new treasures to whirl around to notice the visitors for the first time.

Neal's jaw dropped. His eyes grew wide. Grasping the back of a chair, he held himself up while cocking his head in Mac's direction. Seeming to fear his father was going to fall over, Scott clutched his arm.

The housekeeper appeared out of nowhere to grab Neal's other arm, which startled Mac. He thought she had gone back inside after showing them out to the patio.

Neal was still opening and closing his mouth as if he couldn't find his voice, when Mac explained, "A collector of stolen art recently died and left it to my mother. He had purchased it from a fence shortly after your wife's death."

Neal rushed forward to grab Mac by the shoulders. "Do you have it with you now? Can we have it back?"

David explained, "The statute of limitation on the theft has run out. Legally, it belongs to Mac."

"What do you want for it?" When he saw Mac's surprise, Neal said, "I assume that's why you came to see me. To offer to sell it to me. Well, I want it. Name your price."

Mac reminded him, "You don't even know what condition it's in."

"I don't care," he replied. "Ilysa put her heart and soul into her paintings. That painting was her favorite. It was to be her masterpiece."

Scott said, "It's the only self-portrait she'd ever done."

"You didn't see it," Rachel told her husband. "I didn't think it was that good."

"Still, she painted it for Dad."

Neal's voice deepened. His eyes were still on Mac's. "Whatever you want, I'll pay. No haggling."

Mac could feel David's and Bogie's eyes on him while the determined man ordered him to name his price for something he wanted so badly that money was no object.

The feeling was surreal.

"I didn't come to sell you the painting, Mr. Hathaway," Mac confessed. "It's natural that you'd want it. Frankly, I wasn't thinking about that. I want to help you find out who killed your wife."

It was Neal Hathaway's turn to be shocked. He cleared his throat and blinked several times before saying, "I want that, too. Very much…If I were you, I'd focus on Victor Gruskonov, Ilysa's agent."

Susan added, "He told Ilysa that he was coming that weekend, but none of us saw him."

"He got hung up on a business deal and was coming in later," Neal said. "He was supposed to come in Sunday night, rent a car, and be here to go up to the Inn for breakfast Monday morning. Ilysa was going to let him handle the sale of this painting at the show in Paris, and then that was going to be it. She was retiring."

"Retiring?" Mac asked. "To do what?"

"Be my wife." Neal choked up. "We were going to start a whole new life together. We were going on a second honeymoon and travel all around the world to visit every country. It was going to be a year-long honeymoon. This was to be her last painting. She wasn't going to work with Victor anymore…" He took out a handkerchief to dab at his eyes.

Greta patted his arm.

"But Ilysa ends up murdered and Victor Gruskonov never shows up." Mac slowed down when he saw David's brow furrow. His eyebrows were almost meeting between his eyes.

Nancy was nodding her head. "I don't see where the mystery is. Have you people been looking for Victor Gruskonov?"

"We walked in on him and Ilysa arguing in the kitchen one night a few weeks before she was killed," Rachel said. "Do you remember that, Scott? It was before you went to Europe."

"I do," Scott said. "Ilysa was furious. She was screaming at Victor that it was his fault. Man, I never saw her so mad. She threw him out. She was mad for days after that."

Mac asked, "His fault for what?"

"No idea." Scott shook his head. "I asked her and she refused to talk about it."

Rachel was hugging herself with her arms folded across her chest. "I felt so bad for her. Whatever it was upset her. After that fight, I never saw him again." She asked Neal, "Did you ever see him after that?"

"Only a couple of times," Neal said, "I know what you're talking about. Something definitely happened between them to sever their friendship. Things changed. I asked Ilysa, too. She wouldn't tell me."

Bogie reminded Mac, "Unfortunately, we've never found Gruskonov to question him."

David asked, "What did Victor Gruskonov look like?"

Peyton scoffed, "You're asking that now?"

"He had long hair that he wore in a pony tail and a black goatee. Right?"

Everyone nodded their heads.

"But none of you saw him for weeks before the murder?"

Again, they nodded their heads.

Mac asked them, "Would any of you have recognized him if he cut his hair and shaved the goatee?"

The question was met with a mixture of shrugs and nodded heads.

Bogie told them, "Our BOLO includes a picture of Victor Gruskonov without the beard. We've got that covered."

❧　❧　❧　❧

The sunny studio bore no resemblance to the crime scene that David and Bogie had investigated eight years earlier. The artist studio had been converted into a fitness center with machines, mats, and brightly colored prints on the walls.

"We've had the studio redecorated," Rachel said. "Are you going to be able to reconstruct what happened?"

"We should be able to." Bogie opened his valise to remove a folder filled with crime scene photos. He crossed the studio to the breakfast bar on which rested a collection of fruits and vegetables in baskets. The counter was home to a juicer, blender, and food processor.

David turned to Neal and his son. The rest of their guests had followed them into the studio. "I think it would be best if you all waited outside."

"But what if he has some questions?" Neal asked.

Before David could respond, Mac called over to them, "Who was it that found Ms. Ramsay? Mr. Hathaway? I'd like him to stay. Everyone else should leave."

With disappointed expressions, everyone left and David closed the door behind them.

Neal waited with his back against the wall while Mac leaned up against the breakfast bar to read over the reports in the folder that Bogie had brought with him. On the other side of the breakfast bar, Bogie and David went through the crime scene photos one at a time.

After a long wait in silence, Neal cleared his throat.

"I haven't forgotten about you, Mr. Hathaway." Mac looked up from the report. "Tell me about when you found your wife's body."

Neal glanced from Mac to David and Bogie. After clearing his throat, he began. "It was Labor Day. We were planning to go up to the Spencer Inn for brunch. When I woke up, Ilysa was gone. She liked to come over to the studio at night to paint—when it was quiet. I had assumed she went to bed here when she got tired. So I came looking for her."

"Did she do that often?" Mac asked.

"All the time."

"Would she be alone here when she painted?"

Neal Hathaway stared at him without answering.

"This is a murder investigation," Mac pointed out. "I have to ask."

"We had the perfect marriage," he answered in a strong voice.

"Okay," Mac said. "So you wake up. Your wife is gone. Everyone is getting ready to go out for breakfast. What time was that?"

Neal answered without hesitation. "A little after seven o'clock."

"Tell me about when you got here. Was the door open?"

"No, it was shut."

"Was it locked?"

"No. I just opened it and walked in and there she was in the middle of the floor." He covered his mouth with his hand. His face contorted with emotion. "There was blood everywhere. It was the single worst thing I'd ever seen in my life. You can't imagine."

Envisioning the hundreds of murder cases that he'd worked on during his career, and the effect of loved ones finding the bodies, Mac could imagine. "Was anyone with you?"

"I was alone."

"What happened then?"

"I called over to the main house on the intercom and told Greta that Ilysa was dead and to call the police."

David asked, "What else happened?"

"Silence. Greta asked if I was all right. I remember nodding my head because it was hitting me. I said call the police. Then I hung up and everything became a blur." He looked up from the spot where he had found his wife's body. "I don't think I can be much help after that. I think I went into shock."

Mac asked in a low voice, "How did Scott and Rachel get along with your wife?"

Neal stood up straight at the suggestion of disharmony between his son and his wife. "He loved Ilysa. He was best man at our wedding. We were a very happy family." He warned Mac. "Don't even think of going there in looking for suspects."

Mac shot a grin at David and Bogie over his shoulder. "How about your daughter-in-law?"

The corner of Neal's lips curled. "Rachel has issues."

David recalled, "Rachel was fighting with your assistant, Susan, when I arrived on the day of the murder."

Mac asked, "What was that about?"

Neal shook his head. "Like I said, Rachel has issues. Susan has a few of her own. When you get the two of them together, they both have issues. Throw in Nancy Kaplan and it becomes a hot tub of issues. Ilysa was smart enough to stay out of it. None of them liked that."

Chuckling about Neal's frank response, Mac asked David, "What were Susan and Rachel fighting about?"

"They both said it was nothing. Rachel accused Susan of trying to leave. Susan said she was only packing her car for when she was released to go home."

Mac asked, "When did you notice that the painting was missing?"

Neal's eyes glazed over. "I didn't. While I was waiting for the police to come, I remember Rachel coming in. She screamed, and then she ran downstairs. There was more screaming, and then an air horn…"

"Did anyone else come in while you were waiting for the police?" Mac asked.

After a long silence that seemed to fill the studio with the memory of the death years before, Neal Hathaway shook his head. Tears came to his eyes.

Bogie recalled, "The Kaplans arrived after our people."

Neal found his voice again. "They were staying at the Spencer Inn. When we didn't show up, Nancy called; and Susan told her about what had happened."

Mac stood up from where he had been leaning against the breakfast bar. "You saw the painting the night before?"

"We all did," he said. "Ilysa had been working on it all summer. This was supposed to be her masterpiece. It was going to be publicly unveiled at the Louvre the next month."

"Everyone was here when she unveiled it?" Mac went over to admire the view.

Neal nodded. "Sunday night. After dinner. We had dessert and champagne here in the studio to celebrate."

Mac moved the standing weight scale from where it was set next to the wall to the middle of the room. "Where was the easel when she did her unveiling?"

"It was over closer to the window. Between the windows and the breakfast bar." He coughed. "I didn't want to convert the studio into a fitness room, but Rachel insisted. She said it was a waste to leave it the way it was, since Ilysa was…"

Mac sensed Neal's daughter-in-law permitted only the minimal amount of time for mourning before making a grab for the space—and anything else—for herself.

"Which way was the easel turned?" Using the weight scale as a substitute for the easel, Mac asked Neal about its placement in the room at the time of the murder.

"Facing the center of the room."

"You said everyone was here?"

"All of us. Me. Susan. Rachel. The Kaplans were here, too. Victor was supposed to be here." Neal added in a harsh tone. "I know he did it. He planned it this way."

"How did Victor meet Ilysa?" Mac saw David cock his head as if a thought was nagging at his brain.

Neal's tone was firm. "They grew up together in the same little village in Scotland. When Ilysa started selling her paintings, Victor swooped in to become her agent. But she told me that she wasn't happy doing what she was doing, and she was going to quit."

"Which would have left Victor where?" Bogie asked. "Sounds like a motive for murder."

Neal said loudly, "Exactly!"

After allowing him to leave, Mac compared the crime scene pictures to the room as it was now. It was difficult. When she had remodeled, Rachel ensured the studio was barely recognizable of its former self.

"Her body was here." Bogie gestured at the space on the floor in front of the scale. "Blood splatters started six feet in from the door. We believed her attacker struck the first blow to the back of the head after entering the room."

"There was blood in front of the easel and some cast off around the base," Mac said. "No sign of forced entry. Either the door was unlocked, or she and the killer came in together. But she was in her pajamas and bathrobe."

David said, "The last time everyone saw her, she was going to bed. Neal Hathaway says they went to bed together."

Bogie added, "But he wasn't awake when she left. So he couldn't tell us what time she came to the studio. The time of death was between midnight and one."

"She came over here to the studio," Mac said, "and she gets killed." He went to the windows looking out on the lake to peer out along the shore to the main house. "The top floors of the mansion look right out here. She could have seen the thief stealing her masterpiece and came to stop him."

Bogie said, "That's what we were thinking. She comes in to confront the thief and he bludgeons her to death with the hammer."

"Was the murder weapon hers or his?"

Bogie answered that the hammer used to kill Ilysa had belonged to her.

Walking the path from the door to the middle of the room, Mac stopped and pointed across the room to the kitchen counter located on the other side of the breakfast bar. "According to these pictures, her paints were over there, but she painted over here. That's a long way to go dip a paint brush."

David and Bogie glanced at each other.

"How did I miss that?" Bogie asked.

Frowning, Mac stood over the spot where Ilysa's body had been found. "There's no void in the blood spatters around the easel." He showed Bogie and David the picture of the body on the floor in front of the bare easel. While they studied that picture, Mac handed them the other pictures of the blood on the floor around the easel. "There's no blood on the painting, either. I tested it."

"That means the canvas wasn't near the body to catch any of the splatter," David said.

Mac pointed out, "But the easel was right next to the body."

Bogie said, "If it was on the easel at the time of the murder, there would have been a void in the blood splatter."

"And on the painting," Mac said. "There's neither."

"So where was the painting while Ilysa was being killed?" David turned around as if it may still be in the studio.

"Gone already?" Bogie asked.

Mac showed them another picture of the breakfast bar with an industrial sized roll of wrapping paper resting on the floor next to it. "She was getting it ready for shipping when she was killed. That's why Ilysa had put the paints over there—To make room on this counter to wrap up the painting."

He went into the center of the room to reconstruct the murder. "The killer comes into the room and strikes the first blow several steps into the room. Ilysa manages to cross the room to here—" He stood over the spot where her body had been found. "—where he beats her down to the floor and kills her."

He turned to the kitchenette. "The painting was up here on the counter. It may have already been wrapped up and all the killer had to do was take it." He held up his finger. "Or … it was already gone and not in the studio at the time of the murder."

Bogie asked, "Which was it? Was the painting stolen before or during the murder?"

"That's an important question," David said. "If the painting had already been stolen, then most likely, it's not the motive for the murder."

"If there's no blood on the painting, it's entirely possible that it wasn't even in the room," Bogie said. "That sends the case in a whole different direction."

David and Bogie turned to Mac, who was staring down at the floor where Ilysa Ramsay's body had lay lifeless eight years before. Abruptly aware of their questioning gaze on him, he responded, "I'm working on it."

Chapter Five

"Hey, you," Detective Cameron Gates shouted to Priscilla Garrett, the senior forensics technician in the crime lab, located on the ground floor of the barracks.

It was time for Priscilla's lunch break, which she took as soon as the clock struck the hour and not a minute later for fear of going into nicotine withdrawal.

Cameron's call across the lab stopped the buxom blond from shedding her lab coat and racing in her high heels out the other exit to the corner of the parking lot reserved for smokers. "What are you doing?" The detective sauntered the length of the lab.

"Lunch." As if it were a jar filled with creepy, crawly bugs, Priscilla eyed the brown folder that Cameron had tucked under her arm. "Unless you're here to offer to buy me a salad and bottled water, it's going to have to wait."

Shades of Murder

Cameron considered the suggestion. A refusal would be the wrong answer. Priscilla would be gone, and she'd have to come back later, which was not an option. Now that Jane Doe's murder case was officially taboo, Cameron couldn't risk talking to her when the lab was in full swing with big-eared forensics officers.

That morning at staff meeting, Lieutenant Sherry Bixby had made a big deal about no detectives reopening any cold cases without first clearing them through her. Cameron could feel all eyes on her. No one said the words, but the other detectives on the squad knew about which cold case Sherry Bixby was talking.

The order was meant for her.

Sherry doesn't know me very well, does she? If she's looking for a fight, I'm her girl.

Three hours later, Detective Cameron Gates was in the forensics lab offering to buy Priscilla Garrett lunch in exchange for a favor.

Her purse hanging by its strap off her shoulder, Priscilla asked, "What do you want?" Her low voice resembled a growl.

"I need for you to run a set of fingerprints through AFIS. We need for it to be a broad search to include the international database."

Priscilla shifted her weight from one high heel to the other and cocked her head at the detective. "For that you want to buy me lunch? What's the other half of the equation?"

"It's Jane Doe's prints. Victim Number Four. The Oliver Cartwright case."

"Do you *want* to get fired?" Priscilla shouted before Cameron shushed her.

She pushed the forensics officer back down into her chair. "It's evidence."

"From a closed case," Priscilla said.

"That's a lie. Until her killer is caught, the case is open. It was never closed."

"Bixby says the case is closed. Cartwright did it."

"No, he didn't," Cameron said. "Bixby wasn't on that case. I was. Gregory and I said from the get-go that it was a copycat. Jane Doe was a body dump. Cartwright's murders weren't. Now, I've found in the autopsy report that Jane Doe had European dental work. Suppose she was European? That would explain why no one here has reported her missing? Can you run her fingerprints through AFIS again and check the international database for me?"

A wide grin crossed Priscilla's face. Her plump painted lips parted to reveal bright white straight teeth. "Why do you want to put a bullet in your career?"

"That's not why I'm asking you to run these prints," Cameron said. "Jane Doe was a woman just like you and me." She pointed the corner of the case file at the picture Priscilla had of her teenaged daughter on her desk. "Suppose it was you. Suppose you were found dead in a field and no one bothered trying to find out your name. You just didn't come home one day, and your family never found out what happened to you, because politically it didn't fit into some bureaucrat's agenda." A sly smile crossed her lips. "Making Bixby look bad would be an added benefit."

Priscilla looked around the lab to see how many of the technicians had returned from lunch. Time was ticking away. "How wide do you want me to cast the net?"

Cameron slipped the folder into her hand. "Let's go for broke. Run a full search of the whole database. Thanks, Priscilla. You're doing the right thing."

"Haven't you ever heard that good guys finish last?"

When Cameron turned to leave, Priscilla cleared her throat and held out her hand. "Lunch."

Cameron slipped a ten-dollar bill into her palm.

"Have you seen the prices at Panera Bread lately?"

CB   ಬಿ   ಣ   ಬಿ

"Does he ever blink?" At his desk, Officer Eric Foster clutched his submarine sandwich close to his chest to protect it from Gnarly, who was perched and ready to pounce.

From the moment Spencer's newest rookie officer had taken his lunch from the bag, Gnarly sat motionless like a statue. Refusing to lose sight of his target, he willed the food to come to him.

"Nope." Mac answered the officer while keeping one ear in the direction of Bogie's office where the deputy chief and David were meeting with another officer, Brent Fletcher.

When they had arrived back at Spencer police headquarters, David rushed Bogie into the office to talk to him in hushed voices. Then, they called in Officer Fletcher from where he was out on patrol. A few minutes later, Fletcher retrieved a folder from the file room, and returned to Bogie's office where they closed the door again.

The desk sergeant, Tonya gave up a portion of her attention from a report she was working on to tell Officer Foster, "Gnarly doesn't beg. He demands."

"You can stare at me all you want," Eric told the German Shepherd. "You're not getting my sandwich."

"That's what you think," Mac said. "You'd be surprised how strong his will is."

When the three emerged, David and Bogie were flushed with excitement. Bogie waved a case file over his head. "We found Victor Gruskonov!"

"Where?" Mac asked.

David laughed when he answered, "He's dead. That's why we couldn't find him."

Bogie draped a leg over the corner of an empty desk. "The same morning that Ramsay was found murdered, we got a call about a car submerged in the lake. It had come around that blind corner on Spencer Lane and collided with a six-point buck."

Fletcher added, "Buck went through the windshield. Killed the guy before he hit the water."

"The car had to have been flying," Bogie said. "It turned end over end and landed upside down in the lake."

David explained, "It was a rental car that was picked up at Dulles International Airport on Sunday."

Mac snapped his fingers. "Victor Gruskonov was renting a car and coming out to see Ilysa. That's why you got that funny look in your face when Neal said he was renting a car."

"Exactly!" David was nodding his head.

Bogie said, "No one ever told us during our original investigation that Gruskonov was renting a car."

"That's what happens with cold cases," Mac said. "Little details that witnesses had thought were unimportant come out; and, suddenly, everything gets blown wide open."

"Like today," David said. "When Neal mentioned the rental car, I remembered that this John Doe had his accident the night of the murder—"

Bogie said, "The same night they were waiting for Victor. All this time we've thought he'd slipped in, in the middle of the night, to kill Ilysa and steal the painting—He was dead all along."

Mac asked Fletcher, "Why didn't you know—"

The officer held up his hands. "The guy in the car was using a fake ID. Charles Smith from Miami. We could never identify him. We ran his prints through AFIS and there was no hit."

Bogie said, "This guy had short hair and no beard. He'd changed his appearance and had a different name. But it was him. Now we know. We sent the picture that was on the fake driver's license to the state forensics lab for comparison to our photo of Gruskonov. One and the same."

Mac was shaking his head. "That doesn't make sense. This Victor guy was supposed to be a big wig agent to a famous painter. Why would he be using a fake ID?"

"Doesn't make sense at all," Bogie agreed. "Something certainly is fishy here."

David recalled Neal Hathaway saying that Victor had been held up with some business, which explained his late arrival. "Sounds like fishy business to me."

Mac began pacing. "Was he killed coming or going from the Hathaway place?"

Fletcher shook his head. "The accident happened with him heading north on Spencer Lane. He was heading *toward* Pelican Court, not away."

Bogie told Mac, "That was my first question, too."

"Even if he did kill Ilysa," David said, "He didn't have time to fence the painting and it certainly wasn't in his vehicle."

Mac asked Fletcher, "You're certain the accident was an accident?"

The police officer laughed loudly, "The only way it would have been murder was if that deer was a suicide buck."

"Victor Gruskonov didn't do it," Mac said. "He didn't kill Ilysa and he didn't steal the painting."

"Okay! Here! Take it!"

Their conversation came to a halt when Eric tossed the last of his sandwich, wrapper and all, onto the floor in front of Gnarly, who pounced on it.

Mac said, "I see he broke you down."

"I've never seen a dog like him," Eric said. "No whining. No pawing at me. He just sat there, staring at me like—It's like he was hypnotizing me into giving him what he wanted."

"Which he got," Mac noted.

"Really, Eric? Gnarly hypnotized you into giving him your sandwich?" David chuckled. "He's a *dog*."

While watching Gnarly lick his snout after finishing the sandwich, Eric shuddered. "He's a creepy dog."

ങ ഌ ൙ ൖ

In the corner of West Virginia's northern panhandle, the phone inside the stone house on the cobblestone boulevard of Rock Spring rang at the same time that Joshua Thornton was picking it up to call Cameron Gates.

"Dad, where have you been?" his daughter Tracy demanded to know. Her tone of voice sounded like that of a parent to a child who had missed his curfew.

Joshua was about to report that he'd been out to the store buying ice cream after getting a haircut when he remembered that he didn't have to answer to his children. "I was out."

"Doing what?"

"This and that."

"Dad, I've been calling you all day and getting your voice mail. Then, when I tried your cell, it went straight to voice mail like you had your phone off."

The worry in her voice overriding his rebellion, Joshua said, "I'm fine. Stop worrying about me. I can take care of myself."

Her tone also softened. "I know that, but you aren't as young as you used to be."

Resisting the urge to defend his still youthful status, Joshua assured her that he had been eating regularly; getting a lot of sleep; and, if he was lucky, going out to dinner with a female friend. The doorbell rang after he had hung up from talking to Tracy.

Carrying a pizza box and a liter of soda, Detective Cameron Gates breezed into the foyer as soon as he opened the door. "Man, do I owe you. I think I'm going to have to sleep with you after what I found out today."

When Admiral spotted Irving at the end of the leash hanging from Cameron's wrist, he ducked behind Joshua like the Irish Wolfhound-Great Dane was small enough to hide.

Joshua was still getting over the astonishment that she—and her skunk cat—were there when she thrust the pizza box into his hands. "After ten years, we finally got a break in the case, and it's all thanks to you." She kissed him on the lips.

When she pulled away, she noticed Admiral eyeing Irving, who was twirling around his giant front legs while purring loudly. "Oh, you have a dog." She asked Admiral, "What's your name, big fellow?" Her tone sounded like she expected the dog to answer.

"His name's Admiral. He's a big chicken."

"How dare you say such a thing about such a dignified looking beast." With the dog's chin cupped in her hand, she cooed, "That name suits you. You're a grand and handsome man indeed. I see you met Irving. Irving loves dogs. As a matter of fact, he likes dogs more than he does other cats. I think he believes he is a dog."

Sitting at Admiral's feet, Irving meowed as if to say hello.

While Admiral stared down at Irving with puzzlement on his big face, Joshua reminded Cameron that she had mentioned Irving had issues. "But you never told me exactly what they are. Should I be worried about him?"

"No."

"Since he's in my house I think I have a right to know."

Her nose wrinkled. Embarrassment crossed her face. "Irving suffers from separation anxiety."

Joshua burst out laughing.

She dropped down to detach the leash from Irving's harness. Freed, the skunk cat resumed twirling around Admiral's legs. The dog sucked up enough courage to sniff him.

"Are you serious?" Joshua asked. "Cats don't get separation anxiety."

"It's rare, but some do."

"You have to *care* to get separation anxiety and *cats* don't care."

She sighed with disgust. He could see that she had had this conversation with other people before. "Irving cares. That's why he gets anxious when I leave him alone."

Seeing that he had offended her, Joshua swallowed and forced himself to stop laughing. "What does he do?"

"I'd rather not talk about it." She yanked the pizza box out of his hands and headed down the hallway toward the back of the house. "Where's your kitchen? I forgot to get napkins. I hope you like the works. I got everything on the pizza."

Joshua led her down the hall into the country kitchen at the back of the house. Along the way, she rattled off about her visit to the forensics lab to clandestinely make her request to re-run the prints, and then the call she received later with the news of a hit.

Joshua flipped open the lid of the pizza box to reveal that Cameron wasn't joking about getting everything on the pizza. It was loaded with everything from pepperoni to sausage to ham to pineapple to anchovies.

This is not a woman who worries about her waistline.

"You're a girl after my own heart," he told her. "I can't remember the last time I had a pizza with everything." He went for the plates while she pulled paper towels off the roll to use as napkins.

"You like?"

With an enthusiastic laugh, he nodded his head. "Very much so. With a big family and everyone liking and hating different stuff, I've given up on everything years ago." He served the pizza on two plates while she poured the soda into glasses.

"Don't keep me waiting. Continue. Forensics ran Jane Doe's prints through the international database this time and you finally got an ID. Who is she?"

They sat across from each other at the kitchen table. Sensing that Cameron would be an easy touch, Admiral perched next to her. The Irish Wolfhound-Great Dane's head was above table level. Irving took a spot on the other side of her chair.

"Ilysa Ramsay," Cameron said. "Immigrant from Scotland. You'll never guess who she's married to."

"I hate guessing." Joshua wiped his mouth with the paper towel after a string of cheese that refused to be bitten off dripped down his chin.

"So do I," she said. "So I'll tell you. Neal Hathaway. Big muckity-muck CEO."

He stopped in mid-bite of his second bite, took the slice of pizza from his mouth, and asked, "Ilysa Ramsay? Was she an artist of some sort?"

"I don't know," Cameron shrugged. "All I know is what the AFIS database had in their report and that was from her passport. Scottish immigrant. Came over after marrying an American, Neal Hathaway in early 2003. She was killed *June* 2003—"

Cameron raised her voice to call after him when he jumped up and hurried down the hallway with his pizza in his hand. "—so they weren't married long at all. My question is why didn't he report her missing?"

Seeing that she was now talking to Admiral and Irving, who were both more interested in her food, she picked up her slice of pizza to chase after her host. The animals formed a line behind her. She found Joshua tapping away on the laptop at his antique oak desk in the study. The pizza crust was clutched between his teeth.

She asked, "Is it something I said?"

He took the pizza out to say, "Very much so. Did you look up Ilysa Ramsay?"

Cameron slipped onto the corner of his desk. Her slender legs hung next to his arm. "I only got the ID a couple of hours ago. Priscilla had to call me on the sly when Bixby wasn't around. Why? What do you know about her?"

Joshua slid the laptop around for her to see the screen where a news website announced, "**Artist Ilysa Ramsay Slain**." The date on the article read, September 7, 2004.

For the first time since Joshua had met her, Cameron was speechless. The slice of pizza lay limp in her hand while she stared at the screen. Her brow furrowed. One eye squinted. "They can't be the same person … No way can they be the same person … We have her body and the fingerprints say she's Ilysa Ramsay."

Joshua sat back in his leather desk chair. He entwined his fingers across his chest. A smirk crossed his face. "You, yourself just asked why her husband didn't report her missing. Maybe she wasn't missing."

Cameron hopped down from the desk. The pizza slice flapped in her hand while she gestured. "We have a body and it has Ilysa Ramsay's fingerprints on it." She stopped and stood up straight. "Could immigration be wrong?" Her voice was calm. "Do you know if AFIS has ever made a mistake?"

The thought had never come into Joshua's mind. With no answer coming to his lips, he shrugged. "People make mistakes. Not computer databases."

"I never had this happen before."

Joshua smiled. "What? You never had a murder victim that had been killed before?"

"What do I do?"

Joshua stood up and placed his hands on her shoulders. When his eyes met hers, he had to force himself to keep his mind on track in order not to be pulled into thoughts of kissing her. "Do what you do best. Investigate the case."

"Call Neal Hathaway," she said.

"And ask him what? Why didn't you report your wife's first murder?" He shook his head. "If it were me, I'd call the police investigating the second Ilysa Ramsay's murder to find out how sure they are that they have the right victim."

They turned back to the laptop. Joshua was aware of her hair brushing against his cheek when they squeezed together to read the article.

"Deep Creek Lake," she said. "That's the second address we have the the Hathaways. It's Neal Hathaway's summer home."

"According to this article, that's where his wife was murdered."

"Deep Creek Lake. I've never been there." She turned to him. "Sounds like a great excuse for a road trip."

"There's a wonderful mountaintop resort there that I know you'll love." He moved in closer to her. "It's got a breathtaking view of the lake and mountains." She smelled sweet, like lilacs.

She wrapped her arms around his shoulders. "I'd love to see it sometime."

"I'd love to show it to you." Her eyes pulled him in. "They have a rose garden maze. We can get lost in it ... alone ...together ..."

"What exactly do you have in mind?" Her mouth was close to his. "The two of us ... at this mountaintop resort ... alone ..."

He hesitated. *That's exactly what I have in mind ... What am I doing? I've only just met this woman.*

He pulled back. "Before you go packing, let me do something in this case."

"Besides looking handsome."

His cheeks felt warm. "I'll look into the Ilysa Ramsay murder."

"You've already done that. I gave you a bootleg copy of the case file."

"I'm talking about the second Ilysa Ramsay murder," he told her. "I'll search the Internet for details about that murder. Maybe there are similarities—"

"Other than the victims being the same person," she giggled.

"I'm glad you have a sense of humor."

She sat back down on the desktop. "Most people say I'm crazy."

"Are you sure they're not talking about your cat?" Joshua closed the laptop. "I'll take up the case now. I'll do the background work on the murder in Deep Creek Lake. Then, we'll get together and call the investigator there to compare notes. That way, we can talk intelligently to him about the case, instead of sounding like a couple of ninnies."

She blinked up at him with a mocking expression on her face. "Do I look like a ninny to you?"

Joshua wanted to call her adorable, but instead he took advantage of her being so close to him. He took her face into his hands and kissed her. As if she feared the kiss would end before she wanted, she placed her hands on his. When he started to pull away, she threw her arms around his neck and pulled him back.

"The pizza—" he tried to remind her before she pushed him back down into the chair.

"Irving and Admiral will take care of it for us."

☙ ❧ ☙ ❧

With five teenagers at home, Joshua had managed to keep order in his home with the rule of no sleepover guests of the opposite sex. Since he did little to no dating, he had never had to deal with the issue of wanting his own friend to stay the night.

It was as if Cameron had read his mind before he could issue the invitation. They were eating ice cream on the back porch when she announced, "I need to be getting home." There was a tinge of regret in her voice.

Irving and Admiral had become good buddies. While the huge dog was stretched out to sleep on the porch, Irving had curled up in the crook of his neck to catch a snooze.

"Are…you…sure…you…want…to do…that?" he asked between kisses that started on her forehead, moved to her nose, then each cheek, and ended on her mouth.

With a moan, she paused before saying, "No, Irving and I have to go. We have a stakeout tomorrow morning." As if she feared changing her mind, she jumped up to her feet. "Come on, Irving. Time for us to go home. Say good night to Admiral."

Instantly, Irving was up. Meowing, he fell in step behind her.

That cat does act like a dog.

Joshua escorted her around the wraparound porch to the front of the house and down the steps to her SUV.

After strapping a pet seatbelt around Irving in the back seat and closing the door, Cameron turned around. "I wish I could stay the night."

"So do I," Joshua said. "My son comes back home in less than two weeks. I can't invite you to stay the night then."

"I understand." She took his arms and wrapped them around her waist. "Raincheck? Maybe we'll get lucky at that little place you told me about in Deep Creek Lake."

He held her close. "The Spencer Inn is not little." Together, they leaned against the fender for a long kiss good night.

The quiet little town along the Ohio River was a far cry from the world that Cameron lived and worked in. The sounds of traffic and people racing to and fro were replaced by birds and squirrels squabbling over territory in the trees up and down the block.

He was starting to consider following her home to her bed when he decided to pull back. "I'll call you tomorrow as soon as I find out anything."

"I'll be waiting." While maneuvering the circular drive to leave, she yelled out the window, "Maybe next time you can come to my place. Bring Admiral. Irving loves having friends for sleepovers."

Joshua watched her turn the corner to Fifth Street and roll down the hill to Carolina Avenue, where she would catch Route 30 to take her across the state line and back to Pennsylvania.

His joy at what he could see as the start of an exciting new relationship turned to fear when he saw an unfamiliar black SUV parked across the road. Another advantage to small town living, besides the quiet, is that you know everyone and their cars. He did not recognize this vehicle as belonging on Rock Spring Boulevard.

The headlights turned on. Before Cameron was out of sight, the car pulled out onto Rock Spring Boulevard and followed her down the Fifth Street hill.

Chapter Six

The phone's ringing shattered through Mac's dreams to wake him out of a fantasy about Archie in a shimmery baby blue negligee.

"What in the world—" Mac sprang up in his bed to find the comforter had become wrapped around his legs and waist during the night. The phone's ring resembled an attacking bird's caw while he thrashed about like a butterfly bursting forth from its cocoon.

The phone also disturbed Gnarly, who banged his head twice on the underside of the box springs while trying to crawl out from under the bed where he had made his den.

"What?" Mac snapped into the phone when he was finally able to reach it on the night stand.

The voice on the other end of the line was equally harsh. "Mac, what's going on out there?"

In search of a way to get outside to start his day, Gnarly seemed to join in the conversation with his barks while running from the bedroom door to the windows. With no escape, he jumped up onto the bed to trample his master into releasing him.

"Man alive!" Mac fell out of bed while trying to free himself from the comforter and the dog. "Get out!" Holding the phone to his ear, he ran down the stairs in his bare feet. Gnarly galloped ahead to lead the way. As soon as Mac threw open the door, Gnarly charged out to launch his attack on the ducks at the dock.

"And stay out!" The feeling of the dog's paws fresh on his chest, Mac slammed the door shut.

From the phone in Mac's hand, the caller was still demanding to know, "What's going on?"

Now fully awake, Mac recognized the voice as Ed Willingham, the senior partner of the law firm that his late mother had kept on retainer to handle her estate's legal affairs. "Ed? What's up?" He went into the kitchen to press the button to start his coffee.

"That's what I'm calling to ask you? I just got riled out of bed by a journalist from the Associated Press. What's this about you finding Ilysa Ramsay's lost painting?"

"How does the Associated Press know about that?"

"He got an email from an anonymous source. Is it true? Do you have Ilysa Ramsay's lost painting?"

"Yeah." Mac was surprised by the awe in Ed's tone.

The Massachusetts blue blood that had grown up playing football with the cream of high society—some of the richest and most famous in the country—wasn't easy to impress. "Do you have any idea how much that painting is worth?"

"No, Ed. Do you?"

"Well ..." Stuck for an answer, Ed paused. "I'll make some phone calls to find out. How did you get it?" After Mac had told him about the collector willing it to Robin, the lawyer said, "Then you own it. That's unbelievable."

"It was stolen, Ed."

"The statute of limitations on art theft is seven years. Ilysa Ramsay's painting was stolen eight years ago. Legally, it's yours."

"Legally, but not ethically," Mac said. "I'm giving it to her husband. I'm telling Neal Hathaway today."

"When you say you're *giving* it to him, you're not really giving it to him as in not wanting anything back in return—like a finder's fee?"

"I didn't find it. It was given to me by a less than ethical millionaire, who got his jollies out of hording stolen masterpieces of art simply because he could. Ilysa Ramsay didn't do that painting to be hidden away on a mountain. She painted it for people to enjoy." His coffee brewed and his blood pumping, Mac was now ready to start his day.

"Tell me how you really feel, Mac," Ed said with sarcasm in his voice. "Oh, you are so much like your mother—always doing the right thing and making me feel like a jackass for thinking otherwise."

Mac heard the clink of what sounded like a coffee mug colliding with the receiver on the other end of the line. The clink was followed by a slurp.

Ed asked, "What do you want me to tell the media when they call asking about the painting? This is big news. Whoever leaked this to the media has sent shockwaves throughout the art world. This guy that woke me up asked if you're going to find out who killed Ilysa Ramsay? I assume you're looking into it. I can't see you ignoring a juicy murder case like hers. What do you want me to say?"

Mac poured the coffee into his mug. The perimeter now cleared of ducks, Gnarly scratched at the door. He was ready for his morning biscuit. Mac opened the door and Gnarly led the way to the biscuit jar on the counter.

"Tell them Gnarly and I will be on the case as soon as we're done with our breakfast."

⚃ 耀 耀 ⚃

Cameron needed a shower. After chasing a burglary suspect two-and-a-half blocks through a suburban subdivision in eighty-three degree heat and eighty percent humidity, she was coated with a slick layer of sweat. She felt like her utility belt was going to slip down over her hips and take her slacks with it.

Weeks of stakeout had paid off. The upscale neighborhood had been having problems with a rash of break-ins. All of them occurred during the day while the homeowners were at work. Residents suspected who the culprit was. Detectives from burglary had even questioned the nineteen-year-old troublemaker, who had denied the charges.

Then the burglar escalated things with a home invasion on the widow of a recent murder victim. First, this woman lost her husband to a carjacker, and then her home is violated by a punk, who knew the woman was now alone.

Cameron Gates, the detective working the homicide, ended up on the case whether the detective handling the burglary wanted her or not. No one messes with the family of murder victims whose cases she's investigating.

Cameron was staking out one of the homes in the neighborhood. Every morning, after the owners went to work, she moved in.

When the burglar struck, she was waiting. The right cross he delivered to what he thought was a helpless woman proved to be his downfall.

Now, Cameron was seriously mad.

The perp was running for his life when he went over the back hedge and down the street with Cameron at his heels. When he tripped over a bicycle, she hurtled it without missing a beat.

The chase ended with her tackling him in a freshly mowed front yard. Before cuffing him, she rubbed his face in the cut grass until he looked like the Grinch from Dr. Seuss. It could have been worse. He was lucky she didn't make him eat it, too.

The perp ended up being the very suspect the burglary detectives had questioned.

Filled with the thrill of success, Cameron sashayed across the police parking lot covered in fresh cut lawn clippings, grass stains on her knees and elbows, and sweat from head to toe.

"How does the other guy look?" One of the employees hanging out in the smoking area called out to her.

"Not as good as me," she replied. "I'm not wearing bracelets."

Cameron noticed that a member of the regular crowd was missing. Lieutenant Sherry Bixby spent half of her day in the corner of the parking lot. She claimed she was conducting business with the other smokers; therefore, technically, she wasn't taking breaks.

The detective slowed her pace when she saw Priscilla Garrett turn away. Ironically, she wouldn't have suspected anything if the technician hadn't moved to avoid eye contact so quickly.

Something's up.

Cameron stepped over to the group. "What's up?" she asked them with a chipper tone of voice. She cocked an eyebrow at Priscilla, who kept her head turned away.

"Too bad Irving flunked out of police training," a clerk from human resources chuckled. Smittened with Priscilla, the non-smoker would watch out his office window for when the forensics technician would take her cigarette break to rush outside to the parking lot.

"Only because he intimidated all the canines." Cameron joined in the joke. "While I was out earning money to buy him catnip, he was sound asleep under my desk here at the precinct."

"It's a cat's life," the smoker that had called her over said.

The men wanted all the details about the detective's chase of the burglary suspect, which she gave them in great detail. A talented story-teller, Cameron never failed to entertain them when they asked for the low down on one of her busts. Her audience, consisting of desk-bound support staff, loved to hear about the action from out in the field.

While Cameron told the story, Priscilla quietly puffed away on her cigarette. As soon as she finished, she tossed the butt into the bucket of sand that acted as the community ash tray, gave a short, "Later," and hurried for the door.

"You sold me out," Cameron said in a low voice when she caught up with her. She didn't say it as an emotional accusation, but rather a statement of fact.

Priscilla shot over her shoulder. "I don't know what you're talking about."

Cameron grabbed her by the elbow to whirl her around. "It's all in the eye contact, sweetheart. You may be able to charm everyone here at the station with your soft voice and regal bearing, which was what got you promoted to the senior tech; but I've learned how to look beyond to glitz to see what drives someone's heart. That's right, baby. I've known what you really are from day one. You're a manipulative narcissist that couldn't see beyond your own agenda even if your life depended on it."

Priscilla's eyes narrowed to slits. Through clinched jaws, she asked, "If you really believed that, then why did you ask me to run Jane Doe's fingerprints on the sly?"

"Because I needed them run," Cameron said. "I *hoped* you wouldn't rat me out, but actually I expected you to do it. It's the same way with Irving. Whenever I forget to take out the garbage before going to bed, I hope Irving won't get into it; but I'm not surprised when he does." She let out a laugh. "You and Irving are very much alike. You're both sneaky and focused only on what's going to serve you the best. Only Irving is charming about it."

"I don't need to take this." Priscilla tried to turn away, but Cameron had her by the wrist.

"What was Sherry's reaction?"

Priscilla smirked. "Surprisingly delighted."

"Delighted?"

"Giddy even," Priscilla said. "She asked me if I knew how much money Neal Hathaway had. I could see the wheels turning in her head. By the time she was done with her cigarette, she was almost at a run when she went back inside." Her voice softened when she offered up a consolation. "She's not waiting for you, though. So, you're safe ... for now."

"Where is she?" Cameron asked.

"Gone," she answered with a shrug of her shoulders while tucking the pack of cigarettes down into the case and zipping it shut. "She left about twenty minutes ago when I came out for a smoke."

Cameron was torn between relief that she didn't need to face Sherry and concern that she wasn't there. Sherry Bixby always brought her lunch. She never went out except for office events. Sometimes, she would work through her noon break so that she could leave an hour early for happy hour at one of the bars.

Something's definitely up. I can feel it.

Cameron was still in deep thought when Priscilla jerked her arm out of her grasp. "If you will excuse me, I have to go back into work. Next time you need a favor, don't ask." She shot over her shoulder back at the detective. "Take a shower. You smell like plant fertilizer."

Cameron was playing all the possible scenarios in her head when Priscilla and her smoking companions went inside. A new shift of smokers came out and passed her on their way to the corner.

She's going to muscle her way into my case. She's probably over at Hathaway's place right now interrogating him.

ॐ ॐ ॐ ॐ

120

"You're not going to eat the last bite of that sandwich, are you?" Archie's tone was as accusatory as the glint in Gnarly's eyes staring at the end of the Italian sausage sandwich making its way to Mac's mouth.

Today, a sailing class from the yacht club, located on the next inlet over, was bouncing on the water at the end of Spencer Point. While dining in the shade of the deck umbrella, they watched the students drift along in their brightly colored vessels.

Mac lowered the sandwich. "I was planning to. Why? Did you slip something in it?"

Gnarly uttered a whine mixed with a groan. Archie glanced from Mac to the German Shepherd who inched in closer. The expression in his brown eyes wasn't pleading as much as it was expectation.

"That's why he acts up," Mac said, "because he gets what he wants. If we didn't give in to him—ever—then he'd stop hounding us."

Whining, Gnarly hung his head.

"Mac, how could you?" She slipped her hand onto his wrist when he moved to finish his lunch. "It's only one bite and he's been so good lately. The Belkins had a cookout last night. They served lobster and Gnarly didn't steal even one."

Gnarly uttered a long whine that ended in a high pitched bark. He reached up to paw at Mac's knee.

With her on one side and the shepherd on the other, Mac was surrounded. He tossed the last bite of Italian sausage for Gnarly to catch in mid-air.

"Faraday!" Neal Hathaway's voice was heard to call out from around the corner of the deck.

Unable to believe the influential gentleman was at his home, Mac rose up from the table. "Hathaway?"

Neal jogged around the corner of the house. "Faraday? Are you back here?"

Finished with his sandwich, Gnarly's mouth was empty to allow him to sound off a bark to announce the guest.

"There you are." Seemingly unconcerned about the large dog between him and Mac, Neal hurried across the deck to join them. "Am I glad I found you." He gasped like he had jogged from Pelican Court to Mac's home, which was over a mile away.

Mac asked, "What's wrong?"

"I got a very strange call this morning." Neal dropped down into an empty chair at the table. "I handed it off to Kaplan to handle." With a handkerchief, he mopped sweat that poured down his forehead and neck. It was hard to tell if the sweat was due to the heat or nerves. Mac surmised it was the latter.

"I even called my lawyer to give him a heads up," Neal said, "but the more I thought about it—"

"Would you like some iced tea?" Wrinkles from concern formed across Archie's forehead. She looked like she feared Neal Hathaway was going to have a coronary before their very eyes.

Neal's eyes widened with surprise when he noticed her. With the handkerchief hanging from his chin, he stopped wiping his face. "Hello."

Mac tried to introduce them, but Archie was already running into the kitchen for a fresh glass of iced tea for their guest.

Forgotten, Gnarly jumped up to plant his front paws on the table and stuck his nose into Neal Hathaway's face as if to introduce himself since no one else would.

"This is Gnarly." Mac pulled him down from the table by the collar. "Go steal a beach towel from someone's dock. This is a private meeting."

With a humph noise, Gnarly trotted off the deck and disappeared down the path in the direction of Archie's cottage.

After gulping almost the full glass of tea that Archie served him, Neal was able to continue. "This morning, I got a call from a woman saying that she's investigating Ilysa's murder—"

Mac glanced over at Archie, who shook her head. "It wasn't me."

When Neal looked from her back to him, Mac explained, "Archie does research for me. She had looked up the background on your wife's murder for our investigation."

"But I didn't call you," she asserted.

"No, it wasn't you," Neal replied. "This woman's voice was deep and gravely. It almost sounded like a man's voice."

"She's investigating Ilysa's murder?" Mac asked.

"And with what she's uncovered so far, it could be very embarrassing for me and my company. She could let the case go cold, or she could continue with the investigation, in which case it could prove to be very expensive and messy. The choice was up to me, based on how much I wanted it to cost me."

Archie said, "Sounds like a shake down to me."

"That's exactly what it was," Neal said with relief that he wasn't imagining the purpose of the call. "So I called Peyton Kaplan and gave him the phone number she had given me to call back with my answer. He did a quick check. It was a cell phone number that he couldn't trace because it was one of those throw away phones. But he said he'll take care of it. Then, the more I thought about it—Who was this woman? Why now? Why the shake down? Could she be one of O'Callaghan's people? Maybe she's a dirty cop working for him."

Mac shook his head. "Definitely not one of David's people. He has two women on the force. One is the desk sergeant. Tonya. I know her. She'd never shake down a suspect."

Neal Hathaway's voice shot up an octave. "Suspect? I thought I was a victim. It was my wife that was murdered."

Archie's gentle tone calmed him down. "Mac didn't mean it that way. Clearly, this woman considers you a suspect."

"Everyone is a suspect when there's a murder," Mac said. "None of the women in David's department are directly involved in this investigation. The other woman is a patrol officer. When did this call come in?"

"A little after nine this morning—right after breakfast. Usually I don't answer the phone, but today is Greta's day for grocery shopping. Since she's out all day, I go ahead and answer it. If I hadn't picked up, I doubt if she would've put the call through." He smiled. "She's very good at screening my calls. After fifteen years of working for me, she's excellent at knowing what calls to put through and what ones are crackpots."

"If it was at nine o'clock," Archie noted, "that was more than four hours ago."

"I know," Neal said, "I should have come sooner, but I was going to just let Kaplan and my lawyer, George Scales, handle it; but the more I thought—O'Callaghan called me last night. Victor Gruskonov is dead."

"That's right," Mac said.

His face contorted with emotion. "That means one of my people did it."

"Your people?" Cocking his head at him, Mac fought the grin that came to his lips.

My people. It was a term he had heard bantered about when he was on the police force. "I'll have my people call your supervisor," suspects would say. Mac considered it a joke. The well-to-do considered having people working for them to be as much of a status symbol as a Mercedes or Jaguar. Since his move to Spencer, he had been told more than once, "I'll have my people contact yours to set up a lunch date." To which Mac would reply, "I don't have any people...but I do have a dog."

Neal sat forward in his chair. "All these years I've thought Gruskonov killed Ilysa. If he didn't do it, then it had to be someone who was at the estate that weekend. Kaplan or his wife. Susan. Rachel. My family. My employees. My friends. My people." He choked. "I'm responsible for all of them."

Archie took his hand. "That doesn't make you responsible for her murder. If any of them killed her, it's their fault."

"Could any of them be behind this shake down?" Mac asked him.

"No," Neal said.

Mac was doubtful. "You don't think any of them could shake you down, but they could kill your wife?"

Neal let out a small gasp. "Ilysa used to tell me that I was too trusting. … Why is this person doing this? Now? The painting? The case opening up again? Everything?"

"I think we'll find that this shakedown artist is an opportunist," Mac said. "It's been all over the news about the painting showing up. That has dredged up a rehashing of the murder. So this woman is trying to take advantage of it. Wait for Kaplan and your lawyer to find out what they can, and then we'll see about nailing her for attempted extortion."

Neal wiped his sweaty face again. "I guess you're right. I apologize for running over here like this. I guess I'm jumpy with all this coming up again—It's brought back a lot of bad memories from when Ilysa died." He turned to Archie. "She was the love of my life."

"I can see that you loved her very much. You two must have been very happy." Archie stood up. "Would you like to see the painting? We've moved it down to the study."

The reminder of the painting brought a smile to Neal Hathaway's face. "I would love to." He turned to Mac. "Have you given any thought to my offer to buy it from you?"

Before Mac could answer, Gnarly came galloping up the steps from where he had disappeared earlier. He clutched a beach towel in his jaws. His pace didn't slow when he trotted across the deck and stopped in front of Mac where he dropped the towel at his feet. Gnarly then looked up at Mac with expectation filling his face.

When Mac was unable to respond due to shock, Gnarly barked and sat up on his hind legs. He was waiting for his reward for a job well done.

Neal was impressed. "How about that? You told him to go steal a beach towel and that's what he did. That's one smart dog."

"If he's so smart," Mac replied, "why doesn't he know sarcasm when he hears it?"

☙ ❧ ☙ ❧

"Are you kidding me?" Joshua blurted out his objection when Cameron called his cell to break the news about her suspicions of Sherry Bixby inserting herself into the investigation.

He punched the dashboard of his SUV and cursed. He really liked the teamwork he was developing with Cameron—and it wasn't only romantically. They were in sync—like he'd never had with any partner in the past. There was no room on their team for an obese, obnoxious, chain smoker.

"I don't like it any more than you do, darling," Cameron told him. "I don't even know where she is. Priscilla said she was actually giddy about finding out that Jane Doe was Neal Hathaway's wife and talked about how much money he has. I'm afraid of what she might do."

"She wouldn't!"

"She doesn't think straight," she said. "Everyone has noticed it since she's been plucked down here, but no one has the guts to blow the whistle to have something done. Now, it may be too late."

"Have you tried calling her cell?"

"She's not answering," Cameron said. "I'm searching her office now. Where are you? If I need backup, can you get here?"

"I've got your back, baby."

He had her back more than she knew. He was watching when Priscilla Garrett broke the news of her betrayal. The two women's body language told him that something had gone wrong. Cameron's call served to confirm his suspicion.

Directly across from Joshua's car, two men in a black SUV with Virginia plates had also watched the show.

We're going to have a convoy. Them following Cameron, and me following them.

Joshua climbed out of the back of his car. Keeping low, he made his way to the black SUV, where he threw open the back door and jumped into the back seat.

"You know you'd get more information faster if you flashed your badges, introduced yourselves, and said please," he told the two agents reaching for the guns in their holsters.

"Thornton!" the older investigator said. "Someday you're going to get shot doing that."

"You'd think after thirty years of doing this that you'd be better at tailing people—especially a state police homicide detective."

Seeing that his partner clearly knew the intruder, the younger man relaxed and went back to eating the submarine sandwich and chips he had in his lap.

The older man in the driver's seat introduced him. "Thornton, meet Special Investigator Kenny Hill, he's my replacement. Kenny, meet Joshua Thornton, former JAG lawyer, now small town lawyer."

Kenny wiped his fingers on a napkin before shaking Joshua's hand.

"So Harry Bush is finally retiring, huh?" Joshua asked the driver. "I thought I'd never see the day."

"Seeing the way you keep popping up after you retired what? Eight years ago?" Harry chuckled. "But I thought I'd give it a shot. My wife has been bugging me to move to a mountaintop in Virginia and grow wine." He shrugged. "We'll see."

"This must be your last case. Ilysa Ramsay, I assume."

"Talk about going out with a bang!" Harry laughed. "If I can nail Ilysa Ramsay, then I can go out a legend."

Joshua said, "I assume when AFIS got a hit on Ramsay, some sort of red flag went up. Why was it flagged? What interest does the FBI have in her?"

Before Harry could answer, Kenny announced with his mouth full of lunchmeat, "She's on the move." He pointed with a potato chip. "And she's got the skunk with her."

"I've got her." Harry started the car.

The three men watched while Cameron climbed into her cruiser.

"She still has grass in her hair," Kenny said. "You'd think she'd clean up after tackling that dude a little while ago."

"She's hunting down her boss." Joshua sat back to buckle his seat belt. "She's inserted herself into this case and right now no one knows where she is."

"Everyone and their brother has gotten involved in this case." Harry pulled out of the parking space to fall in behind her police cruiser. "You do know your girlfriend's crazy?"

"She's not crazy. Her cat is."

"Cat? I thought that was a skunk," Kenny said.

"He thinks he's a dog." Joshua asked Harry, "Why do you say Cameron's crazy? What do you know about her?"

"When that flag went up, I got backgrounds on everyone involved," Harry explained. "Detective Cameron Gates. Widow."

"Widow?" Joshua replied. "She was married?"

"Only for about four months," Harry said. "Very sad. It was seven years ago. Her husband was a state trooper. He pulled over a guy for a routine traffic stop and got run over by a drunk driver that sideswiped him and the car he pulled over. Gates lost it."

"Do you blame her?" Swallowing, Joshua understood why she never mentioned it.

"After months of one issue after another," Harry said, "she took a year off from the force. Disappeared off the radar. Then she came back and has become a top cop. Only one reason she's not in charge."

"What's that?" Joshua asked.

"She's crazy," Harry and Kenny answered in unison.

When he received no more details about their claims, Joshua went back to the case that had brought them in to tail Cameron Gates. "What interest does the FBI have in an artist?"

"If she was just an artist, nothing," Harry replied. "Ramsay is more than an artist."

"A spy?"

"I wish," Harry said. "She and her partner stole classified information and *sold* it to the highest bidder—the winner in this auction being Al Qaeda."

"And Neal Hathaway's company puts up satellites that collect defense information," Joshua said.

"Some of the most sensitive information pertaining to Unites States defense," Harry said. "If Al Qaeda got their hands on it …" He shook his head.

"Is Neal Hathaway aware of what his late wife did?" Joshua asked.

"We could never prove anything," Harry said. "She and her partner are that good."

"Who's her partner?"

Finished with his sandwich, Kenny pointed up ahead with his rolled up wrapper. "She's turning into that little airport."

Up ahead, the cruiser turned off the four-lane freeway onto Darlington Road, a two-lane access road to enter Beaver County Airport, a small county-owned public airport.

The cruiser was turning into a gate leading to a private hangar when a black Jaguar came racing around the corner of the building to threaten a head-on collision. Cameron veered to the right so hard the the tail-end of her SUV whipped around to send her into a one-eighty turn.

Harry had enough warning to swing the steering wheel in order to pull out of the way of the Jaguar, which flew out the gate and down the road.

"Talk about a bat out of hell!" Kenny yelled.

"What was chasing him?" Joshua turned around in time to check out the Jag's Pennsylvania license plate. It read *SCALES*.

"Must be late for a meeting," Harry said. "Hathaway has a couple of his company jets here."

Kenny told Harry, "Hang back. She's going to see us."

"Do you think so?" Harry said with sarcasm. "Like she would have missed us just now."

"That's okay." Joshua was dialing on his cell phone. "She wants me to back her up." When Cameron picked up, he said, "I'm in the black SUV behind you with a couple of friends. What's up?"

She answered, "I did some old fashion gum shoe stuff and found where Sherry had written on a notepad to meet a secret informant from Hathaway Industries here at the airport hangar to talk about the Ramsay murder. You would have been proud of me. I scribble across a used notepad to pick up the impressions from the note before. It said:

Hathaway
Beaver Airport
Hangar #3.
1:30.

She added, "I'm so good I scare myself."

Joshua checked the time on the clock dashboard. It was quarter to two. "We're late. The meeting's over."

A black Chevy with a dented rear fender was parked along the side of the airplane hangar. "Her car's still here." She pulled up beside it.

Joshua hung up the cell. "You might as well pull in next to her. I think your cover's blown."

After they climbed out of the car, Joshua introduced them to Cameron.

Irving stuck his head out of the cruiser's open window. Seeming to determine that the two agents weren't worthy of his attention, he curled on the passenger seat to go back to sleep.

Kenny noted the grass that hung from Cameron's shaggy locks.

"How old are you?" she asked him.

While the young agent hesitated, she looking him up and down before smirking. "When you're forty years old, I'd like to see you chase a nineteen-year-old perp two blocks and tackle him." She pointed at the grass stains on her clothes. "These are badges."

Agreeing, Harry told her, "He'll learn."

Her hand on her gun, Cameron went around to the front of the airplane hangar where the doors were closed. "Sherry," she called. "Bixby. I know you're here."

Joshua drew his gun from his belt holster and followed her. The two FBI agents drew their guns and split up
to go around to the other side of the building.

No cars or trucks were parked around the hangar reserved
only for private jets belonging to Hathaway Industries. Since
flights weren't regularly scheduled, the hangar was vacant unless
Neal Hathaway or one of his executives was traveling.

Joshua said, "Where did that Jag come from? If he'd just
come in from a flight, then the pilot and other personnel would
still be here."

"Maybe he was rushing from a meeting, instead of to one."
In front of the building, Cameron placed her hand on the door-
knob to test it. It was unlocked. She pushed open the door and
dropped back. "Sherry, are you in there?" The only response was
the call and flapping of birds up in the rafters.

Joshua gestured that he would cover her while she went
inside.

Her gun pointed to the ground, Cameron hurried inside.
"Bixby." Her voice bounced off the far walls and the two jets
parked next to each other. Tables, boxes, racks filled with a wide
assortment of tools, equipment, and supplies lined the building.
After the echo faded into the rafters, they listened to silence.

The two FBI agents came in behind them. "I think we
missed your boss's meeting," Kenny said.

"I guess so." Cameron turned around. "She must have gone
with them."

She stopped when she saw the blood splatter at eye level on
the file cabinet next to her. "Blood."

It was all she needed to say to signal for them to go back on
alert.

Her attention now piqued, Cameron darted her eyes left to right and up and down. No longer focused on finding her boss, but the source of the blood splatter, what she had missed before now caught her notice. A cast off to the left led to the splatter on the ground and around the corner of a row of shelving, where it grew in volume in conjunction with the attack's intensity. The blood splatter turned into a trail that ended in a pool where Sherry Bixby had collapsed face down with her head, neck, and shoulders bashed in.

Soaked in blood, the sledge hammer that had done the deed rested between her motionless feet.

"Oh geez!" Cameron lowered her gun.

Kenny choked down the lunchmeat that fought its way back up.

"She didn't even pull her weapon." Cameron noted the gun that was still in its holster on her thick waist. "She completely walked into this with no backup. Stupid self-serving bitch got herself killed."

She pulled out her phone to make the call. While listening to the ring at the other end of the line, she turned to Harry, who was holstering his gun. "What interest do you guys have in Ilysa Ramsay's murder?"

"We're interested in what she was doing when she got killed." Harry cocked his head at her. "What interest does a Pennsylvania State Police detective have in a Spencer, Maryland, murder? This isn't your jurisdiction."

"Huh?" Cameron replied. "We're investigating the murder of Ilysa Ramsay that happened here."

When emergency picked up, she turned away to report a police officer down.

Now it was the FBI's turn to be confused. Harry found himself alone in his disbelief while Kenny went outside to lose his lunch.

Joshua said, "We need to have a meeting of everyone involved in all these murders to get everyone on the same sheet of paper."

Chapter Seven

"There you are." David O'Callaghan found Mac enjoying a before-dinner cocktail with Archie in the Spencer Inn's lounge. In the corner booth reserved for the inn's owner, they were sharing a cozy moment alone when the police chief slid into the seat across from them and cleared his throat. "I've been looking all over for you."

Another part of Mac's inheritance, the Inn rested at the top of Spencer Mountain, which was named after his ancestors, the town's founders. The front of the stone and cedar main lodge offered a view of the lake below and the mountains off in the distance. While resting between boating, golf, skiing, mountain biking, hiking, or any of the other activities, guests could take in the view from the wrap-around porch. They could also partake of refreshments in the outdoor café on the multi-level deck, among the flora of an elaborate living maze; or, if the weather was too chilly, the lounge inside. For more formal eating, the Inn's five-star restaurant offered legendary dining experiences.

More than a year after his inheritance, Mac was still trying to wrap his head around being able to enjoy all of the luxuries of one of the country's finest resorts without ever receiving a bill.

"I returned the beach towel to its rightful owner," he told the police chief.

David cocked his head at him. "What?"

Seeing that he wasn't there about Gnarly, Mac backtracked. "Nothing."

"We've got company on this case."

"Who?" Mac hated it when others horned in on what he considered to be his cases. Usually, it would end up in a tug of war over who got credit for the collar. If the case went cold, then it would turn into a blame game. In either instance, it would not end up being a good thing, especially if it involved the feds.

"Pennsylvania state police and the FBI."

"FBI?" Archie turned to Mac. "The FBI is big."

"Real big." Mac's eyes were equally wide. "What interest does the FBI have in a Scottish artist?"

David gestured at a group coming into the lounge. Bogie was in the lead with two men in suits, who Mac guessed to be the FBI. A woman wearing a state police shield and gun, and man with silver hair, came in behind them. Mac tagged her as the Pennsylvania state police.

That leaves the dude with the silver hair. Where does he fit into all this? Another state police detective? Where's his badge? Nah! He doesn't look like a cop. He's either military or a lawyer.

David told Mac, "Maybe it's best if we all meet in one of your conference rooms. From what I understand, this is complicated."

CB ED CR ED

The second floor executive conference room provided a view of the ski runs. During the summer months, the ski slopes' service road acted as a mountain bike trail.

After introductions were made, Joshua Thornton asked Mac, "How does a millionaire inn owner get involved in a murder investigation?"

"Very carefully," he replied. "How does a small town lawyer get mixed up with the FBI?"

Joshua glanced over at Cameron, who was eying Archie with suspicion. "How else? I met a woman."

Casting a look at Archie, who was equally curious about the female detective dressed in clothes covered with grass stains; Mac said, "I know the story well."

David recounted for Joshua and Cameron about Mac receiving the painting from the art collector. "It was stolen the night Ilysa Ramsay was killed in her studio in September of 2004."

Cameron disagreed. "According to the fingerprints lifted from a body found in Pittsburgh, Ilysa Ramsay was killed in June 2003."

Mac said, "That's not possible."

Cameron bristled at the suggestion that they were wrong. "It's not possible for your murder victim to be Ilysa Ramsay because AFIS says we've got her body."

At the head of the table, Harry Bush, who had taken it upon himself to lead the meeting, held up both of his hands and called for an end to the debate. "Maybe it is possible." He asked David, "Did you run the prints you took from your body through the database?"

David turned to Bogie, who shook his head while answering, "We had no need to. We had a positive ID that it was Ilysa Ramsay."

"From her husband," Cameron pointed out. "Have you considered the possibility that Neal Hathaway killed the real Ilysa Ramsay and dumped her body, and then got a duplicate to take her place? When he got tired of her, he murdered her. Since he was out of duplicates, he had no choice but to report the second murder. When my boss called him on it today, he killed her."

"When and where was your boss killed?" Mac asked.

"Around one-thirty at the Beaver County Airport in Pennsylvania."

Mac and Archie shook their heads. "Not possible," she told her. "Neal Hathaway was with us at one o'clock."

Cameron said, "He's a very rich man. He could have hired someone to kill her while using you two for alibis."

"I don't think Neal Hathaway would do that." Archie continued to shake her head. "I can't believe he would have kill his wife."

Cameron looked across the table at her. "And I find it hard to believe that he wouldn't notice that his wife was suddenly a different person."

"I can offer another possibility," Harry said in a loud voice. "I don't believe Neal Hathaway had any knowledge of this."

David asked, "Tell us how Ilysa Ramsay was killed twice."

"Ilysa Ramsay was two people."

They all stared up the table at Harry, who chuckled back at their stunned expressions. He tucked his thumbs in the waistband of his pants. "Ilysa Ramsay had an identical twin sister. They made a career, illegal as it was, out of being one and the same. They were both exceptional artists, and con women."

Archie asked, "But Ilysa Ramsay … or her sister, was so talented. Her paintings—"

"They started stealing and conning people back before they—Ilysa—became famous. Her sister's name was Fiona, by the way. Good luck in finding a paper trail of her. The two of them assumed one identity—Ilysa—and deleted Fiona's identity. Whichever one's fingerprints they used for the passport under Ilysa's name was obviously the one whose body was found in Pennsylvania."

Joshua said, "Our Ilysa Ramsay had her appendix removed."

"So did ours," Bogie said.

The senior FBI agent laughed. "How's that for being dedicated to the con? When one of them had to have hers removed, her twin had hers removed, too—all so that they could be as alike as possible."

"Why?" Archie asked.

Harry explained, "When you're an artist—especially a beautiful and charming artist—the rich and powerful flock to you and welcome you into their world. While Ilysa was still a starving artist, she decided to take advantage of it. While she would be charming them in the parlor, her identical twin sister would slip in and steal whatever she could from a safe or off a computer. If anyone saw her, Ilysa would have a roomful of guests to alibi her. They would then give the stolen goods to their agent, who was really their fence, who would sell it to the highest bidder."

"Victor Gruskonov," Bogie said.

Harry nodded his head.

"Who happens to be dead."

Harry blinked down the table at the police officer. "When?"

Bogie reported about the John Doe, who had died in a car accident the night of Ilysa's murder.

Harry was still digesting this information when Cameron said, "The Ghost must have been the twin. When Ilysa's picture was all over the news, Fiona started calling me to ask for information about the murder so that she could figure out who'd killed her sister."

Joshua said, "She couldn't go public about it because the FBI was after her."

Harry said, "We could never get enough evidence to nail her. Since we didn't know Ilysa was already dead, when Fiona was killed in 2004, we've been looking for the twin and Gruskonov. We learned in the underground that something big having to do with U.S. defense satellites was going down. We knew it had to be connected to Ramsay and Gruskonov. We almost had him in Germany, but he'd managed to slip away."

David said, "That's why he was using a stolen ID when he had his car accident. He had to in order to get into the United States to pick up..." his voice trailed off.

"Ilysa's painting," Bogie said, "which was stolen when she was killed. That's why she was murdered. She was killed for whatever it was Gruskonov was supposed to pick up."

Bogie's bushy eyebrows met between his eyes and his mustache almost went up his nose when he turned to the special agent. "If you were on this case back in 2004, why didn't you bring this information to us then? If we knew all this, we would have taken this investigation in a whole different direction."

"We had our reasons," Harry said.

Joshua's tone was calm. "You didn't want Hathaway to know that you were investigating his company."

The special agent said nothing.

"Do you suspect Hathaway of being in on the theft?" Mac asked.

"Not him."

"Who?" David asked.

When the FBI agent hesitated, Bogie demanded an answer. "It's time we lay all of our cards on the table."

"Peyton Kaplan has been hiding large sums of money in a secret account in the Cayman Islands for years," Harry said. "The account was opened around the time Hathaway married Ilysa and we have no idea where the money is coming from. If Ilysa had help inside the company, Kaplan would've been the ideal accomplice."

"We didn't know that." Bogie grinned. "Thank you for sharing." His gratitude was mixed with sarcasm.

Harry held up his hands again to keep their attention. "But our sources say the deal never went down. We want to make sure we intercept that information before it gets out. Even after all these years, if what they stole got into the wrong hands—"

"Ilysa or Fiona weren't killed for the stolen secrets," Mac said. "If the transaction was never completed, then that can't be the motive for the murders."

Bogie asked, "Who was killed here in Spencer? Ilysa Ramsay or her sister Fiona?"

"Fiona," Harry said. "I'm fifty percent sure."

Joshua said, "Which will make it difficult to prosecute when we do catch the killer because we won't have any positive ID on the victim."

"Let's worry about that when we catch our killer," David turned to Cameron and Joshua. "Tell us about the murder committed today."

"Lieutenant Sherry Bixby," Cameron reported, "the chief of the homicide squad that I work with. She was bludgeoned to death with a sledge hammer at the airport hangar where Hathaway Industries keeps their corporate jets."

Bogie said, "Same way Ilysa Ramsay the second was murdered. Bludgeoned to death with a hammer."

"Now we're getting somewhere," Joshua said. "Same MO for both Bixby and Ramsay the second. Points to the same killer."

Cameron said, "But Ilysa Ramsay the first was garroted with something thin, possibly a piano wire."

"With all due respect," Mac asked, "could your boss have been trying to shake down Neal Hathaway? Offering to let the murder investigation of his wife go cold in exchange for …" He was startled by the lack of surprise, or offense, on her face.

She regarded him for an instant before replying, "Very possible."

Mac told her, "Hathaway came to my home this afternoon to tell us that he'd gotten a call shortly after nine from a woman saying that she was investigating his wife's murder—"

"I thought Hathaway didn't know about his wife's first murder—" She countered before correcting herself, "I never had a chance to meet with Sherry about what we'd uncovered. She didn't know about the second murder."

Joshua said, "So when Bixby told Neal Hathaway that she was investigating his wife's murder, he would have assumed she was talking about the murder here in Spencer, because he never knew about the earlier murder."

"Because his wife's twin most likely took her place before he realized she had been killed," Mac said.

Archie said, "When he came to see us, he thought the call came from the Spencer police. He had no idea that the call came from Pittsburgh, and your boss was talking about a murder that'd happened earlier."

Cameron told them, "Sherry called Hathaway's home in Mount Lebanon from a disposable cell phone that she'd acquired from vice. What we've uncovered so far, Hathaway's calls there were automatically forwarded to his home here. I doubt if Sherry knew that. Like him, she thought he was in the local area."

Joshua continued, "Sherry then got a call back from a disposable phone to arrange the meeting at the airport where she was killed. We got that from the call records on the cell we found on her body."

"We saw a black Jag leaving the scene," Cameron said. "Do any of your suspects drive a black Jag?"

David and Bogie shook their heads.

"We didn't know about Ramsay's murder in Pittsburgh, either," Harry said, "Somehow, her twin realized she was missing and took her place before anyone knew."

Cameron was still doubtful. "If an imposter took your wife's place, wouldn't you know she wasn't the same woman?"

"Maybe he didn't want to know," David said. "I was there at the crime scene for Ilysa Ramsay the second. Neal Hathaway did not kill his wife—either of them."

Harry cleared his throat. "One thing we can't forget is that the Ramsay twins and Gruskonov stole and were selling sensitive information pertaining to government defense satellites. As far as we know, it's hidden away someplace. If it gets into the wrong hands, there's no telling what could happen."

"What kind of secrets are we talking about?" Cameron asked.

"As Hathaway's wife, Ilysa Ramsay or Fiona, had access to his office, computer, anything. Not only were they both talented artists, but they were also accomplished hackers. No matter which one it was, if she got access to any computer connected to Hathaway Industries, it would have been a piece of cake for her to break into his company's files."

Kenny said, "According to our information, Al Qaeda had won the bid for programs and access codes that would give control of Hathaway's satellites to whoever used them. Use your imagination about what would happen if they got their hands on that type of stuff."

"Basically, *our* satellites would become *their* satellites," David said.

"Exactly," Harry said.

"Is it possible that without her twin, Ilysa was never able to accomplish her mission?" Mac asked.

David recalled, "Neal Hathaway told us that Ilysa told him that this was her last painting, and then she was getting out of the business. She was turning this painting over to Gruskonov to sell and then she was retiring. Translation: This was her last big score."

Mac said, "Gruskonov died before he made the pick-up."

Bogie said, "But someone picked up that painting."

Harry said, "Yet, the deal never went down."

Archie said, "We can't forget that Ilysa Ramsay was a famous painter, even if she was a thief. The painting could have been stolen because of its artistic value."

"The codes are probably still with the painting," Harry said. "Where is it?"

Mac answered, "My place."

Spencer Inn manager, Jeff Ingles burst into the room. "Mac, there's been an explosion at your house."

Chapter Eight

"My boat!" At the sight of his new speed boat, still tethered to the dock next to the boat house, engulfed in flames; Mac held his hands to his head and screamed.

The cause of the inferno was made evident by the white panel van resting directly on top of the boat. They resembled two matchbox toys, one stacked on top of the other. The headlights from the emergency vehicles illuminated the path the van had taken, in reverse, through the floral gardens and down to the dock, where it appeared to have been launched to land on top of the speed boat. The surviving flowers now fell victim to the two fire trucks hosing down the double-decker.

The red, orange, and yellow flames created quite a show. The odd scene had attracted an audience, both on land and the lake.

"They only delivered it five days ago." Mac shook off David, who attempted to hold him back from the scene. "I only had her out on the water one day. She still had three-quarters of a tank of gas."

"It's only a boat." Joshua grabbed him by the shoulders. "Be thankful that no one was hurt."

Bogie emerged from the fire fighters down on the dock. "Sorry about your boat, Mac. She looks like she was quite a beaut."

Mac didn't like the angry stammer that crept into his tone. "Wh-what happened?"

"They think the guy was drunk or crazy or something," Bogie said.

David observed the tire tracks through the landscape. "It looks like he drove in reverse through the gardens and across the dock to land right on top of your boat."

Mac scoffed. "Do you think so?"

Kenny told Harry, "I ain't never seen nothing like this. Have you?"

"Never," Harry said. "Now I've seen everything."

Bogie reported, "Witnesses said he peeled down over the hill like he was being chased by Satan."

"Was he hurt?" Mac finally thought to ask.

"Some boaters fished him out," the deputy chief reported. "He's on his way to the ER now. He was babbling about being attacked by a werewolf trying to kill him."

"Gnarly! I'm going to kill you!" When Mac turned to run up to the house he tripped over an uprooted rose bush and fell face down into a mound of fertilizer.

David helped him to his feet. "Mac, you need to calm down."

"Don't tell me to calm down. Your boat didn't get blown all to hell."

"I'm sure there's a good explanation."

"I'm sure there is, too. Its name is Gnarly."

As Mac stumbled up to the house, Cameron turned to Joshua. "So this is how the rich and famous live."

Joshua nodded his head. "Very much so."

Mac charged up the porch steps and threw open the front door. The rug in the middle of the room was pushed up against the fireplace. Furniture was overturned, except for the loveseat that rested with its back to the door.

Mac found Archie standing guard over Gnarly's favorite chair. "What did you do now, you—"

Archie met him halfway across the room to stop him with a hand on his chest. "Don't you touch him."

"My boat—my house!"

"Bullet hole in the grandfather clock." She released her hand from his chest to point a pink-tipped finger at the clock that had stopped working the hour before due to the bullet that went through its face.

The fury dissolved. As it did, Mac's vision cleared. The roar of his anger silenced enough for him to hear the whine from the loveseat behind her.

Gnarly peered over the back of the couch at him. His ears stood tall and erect. His eyes met Mac with a glint that he had seen many a time—usually right before he snatched a sandwich from his plate.

"He was defending our home," Archie said.

When she turned around, Gnarly's ears fell back and his eyes grew wide and soft while he uttered a mournful whine.

I don't believe this! Gnarly's playing the poor puppy card!

She slipped onto the loveseat next to the dog. "Poor, Gnarly. It must have been quite a fight going up against someone with a gun. What a dog."

Gnarly wagged his tail so hard that Mac could hear it slap the seat cushion.

"You must have been scared, huh?" She pulled his head against her chest into a tight hug. "I don't know what I would have done if he had shot you. You poor helpless dear." Her eyes misted up. "I'm never leaving you home alone ever again." She ordered, "Mac, tell him he's not in trouble."

"I'm not so sure that he's not. Was all this damage necessary?"

"He was doing his job."

When Gnarly turned his head from where he was nuzzling her neck, Mac swore he saw the dog wink at him.

"Mac, how can you be so hard-hearted? The burglar shot at Gnarly. What if he'd been hurt or killed?"

Can't you see he's a con-dog? He's got you wrapped around his dew-claw and he knows it.

She gestured at a sliver of free space on the loveseat on the other side of the dog. "Mac, sit down and tell Gnarly that he's a good dog and how glad you are that he's okay."

Gnarly welcomed his touch by nuzzling him in the chest when Mac slipped onto the couch. "Looks like you had quite a party this afternoon while we were gone, huh, Gnarl?"

Archie stroked the dog's ears. "What happened? Did you chase the bad guy away?"

Gnarly pulled away, stood up on the seat, and dug at the cushions.

Mac told her, "Witnesses said the guy was whacked out. He was probably too drunk or stoned to hit the broad side of a barn."

Gnarly dug his snout deep down between the cushion and the back of the loveseat.

"He told the rescuers that a werewolf was trying to kill him."

Gnarly lifted his snout up from between the cushions with a semi-automatic pistol in his mouth.

 C   D   C   D

"So this is what all the fuss has been about all these years?" Kenny asked when they went down to the study to examine Ilysa Ramsay's last painting.

Bogie handed out evidence gloves to all of them. "Like we really need them now. As much as this thing has probably been handled all these years, any evidence that was on it has already been contaminated."

Mac disagreed. "Remember it was stolen. Poole could allow only a limited number of people to see it. It isn't like this thing has been hung up on the wall at the local gallery. If there's evidence on it of the murder, it could still be on it."

Cameron and Joshua gazed at the image of the woman on the lounging chair.

Joshua said, "That's our victim. But is it Ilysa or Fiona?"

Cameron stepped up to examine the red choker. "The red choker is where she was garroted." She turned to Joshua. "This proves it. Her twin was the Ghost." She pressed her finger against the face and traced the neck and choker in the painting. "This is almost a duplicate of the pictures they showed on the news."

"Even the sofa," Joshua pointed out. "The clover pattern represents the field where the victim's body was dumped."

"Ilysa wasn't predicting her death in this painting," Mac said, "she was trying to flush out her sister's killer by depicting her murder."

"In our last phone conversation, the Ghost told me that she knew who did it," Cameron said, "and that she'd take care of it."

Bogie said, "Instead the killer took care of her."

"The murderer must be in this painting." Joshua stepped back to get a better view.

Everyone lined up on either side of him to study the party scene.

"The first murder victim was garroted." Joshua asked Cameron, "Didn't you say the Ghost asked if the murder weapon could have been a piano wire?"

When Cameron nodded her head, David pointed out that Susan Dulin and Peyton Kaplan were at the piano.

Archie told them, "There's also a harp in the picture. That uses the same type of wire."

"Who's the creepy woman playing it?" Cameron asked.

"Greta," David said. "She's been working for the Hathaways since Neal's son was a little boy."

Cameron shuddered. "She looks like a female version of Lurch from *The Addams Family*."

"The Hathaways have both a piano and a harp," Mac said. "His executive assistant, Susan, plays the harp."

David pointed out, "But she's not playing it in this painting. She's with Peyton Kaplan."

Grumbling, Harry shook his head. "Artists. Using all this symbolism. If she really wanted her sister's killer caught, she should have just told us who did it. But she'd gotten herself in so deep being a thief, that he's still on the loose. Not only that, but if she did steal those access codes for Hathaway's satellites, a lot of innocent people could very well get killed."

Cameron asked Harry, "What exactly are we looking for? A code? A disk? A piece of paper?"

"Could be anything."

While they circled the canvas, Archie bent over to peer at the stretch bars across which the canvas had been stretched. "We're dealing with satellites. That tells me that we're talking about computer data and files."

Mac told them, "Archie is my IT girl."

"I think we're looking for a smart disk." Archie held out her hand. "Mac, can you get me the letter opener from the desk?"

While Mac went to the desk, she dug her fingers down into the corner of the canvas where two bars were stapled together. After he handed the letter opener to her, she dug the point into the opening.

"Careful," Kenny warned.

With a cry, Archie yanked her hand back and held up a smart chip encased in a plastic cover. It was only about one inch by one inch in size. "It may be small, but I'll bet it's filled with lots of secrets."

Harry snatched it from her hand. "Where can we check it out?"

Archie led them over to the desk where Mac's laptop rested.

"Very clever," Kenny told them. "If the painting is X-rayed, a disk that small will be concealed by the staples and nails in the frame."

Harry said, "Once the painting's overseas, the disk is removed and handed over to the buyer."

Archie turned the laptop around for Harry and Kenny to examine the contents of the disk. After examining the list of files on the disk, Harry jabbed Kenny in the ribs. "We got it. Now, I can retire in peace knowing that this information isn't in the lunatics' hands."

Harry popped the disk out of the laptop. "Exactly what we want to protect." He chuckled as he made a show of dropping the disk into an evidence envelope. "I can't wait to call Washington about this. A lot of people are going to be very happy."

Harry let out a gasp when David O'Callaghan caught the disk in midair and tossed it over to Bogie. "This is evidence." The police chief pointed over to the painting. "So is that. This disk and that painting are both going down to the police station to be locked up in the evidence locker." He turned to Mac. "Sorry, but I should have taken this into evidence when it first showed up here days ago. I thought so many years after the murder that it wasn't necessary. But, after what happened tonight—"

"And the direction this case has taken," Bogie agreed.

"—we can't take anymore chances."

Harry argued, "That disk contains information that is extremely important to national security."

"Which is why I'm having it locked up," David said.

Bogie added, "We'll call in additional officers to guard it, along with local, state, and federal officers."

"The safest place for it right now is the police station," David assured him. "We'll protect it."

"But from who?" Joshua asked, "We still don't know who was behind this attack tonight. Was it Ilysa Ramsay's killer or Al Qaeda trying to pick up what they paid for back in 2004."

Harry said, "Fortunately, whoever stole this canvas must have taken it for the painting itself."

Mac said, "The theft of the painting could very well be the motive for the second Ilysa Ramsay murder. The buyer came to pick up the painting, only it had already been stolen, along with the chip. They didn't believe Fiona or Ilsya that she didn't have it. Al Qaeda thought she was cheating them and killed her."

"Without ever getting the chip?" Archie asked.

As if to remind them of his presence, Gnarly barked.

Looking over at Gnarly, who was sitting on the stairs, Joshua said, "It's been all over the news about the painting turning up again. Maybe the buyer tried to collect it tonight, but didn't count on your dog being so ..."

"Brave." Archie jabbed Mac in the ribs before he could use another word. "Bad guys never stand a chance when Gnarly's on the case."

Chapter Nine

"Mac, you're not going to believe what the clerk just told me." Jeff Ingles, the Spencer Inn's manager, rushed across the lobby to meet Mac when he stepped into the lobby.

After dropping Archie and Gnarly off at the entrance, Mac had parked his car and went inside to find the manager in the middle of fit. "After the day I've had," Mac replied, "I'll believe anything."

When Mac didn't stop, the manager fell into step beside him. "Were you aware that the guests you instructed us to place in a corner suite have a skunk with them?"

His voice rose from a dignified low tone to a high-pitched gasp. "Is that Gnarly?" The sight of the German Shepherd at Archie's side made Jeff forget all about the black and white creature in Cameron Gates's arms.

Cameron and Joshua had been content to stay in the pet-friendly roadside hotel in which they had checked-in with Irving on the way into Spencer. However, Mac's offer of a corner suite at the Inn, as his guests, was too good to pass up.

It was a perfect turn of events.

Joshua had offered to let his cousin Tad, who was taking care of Admiral, cat-sit so that they could spend a couple of nights at the Spencer Inn. As much as she wanted to spend a couple of nights alone with her lover in crime, Cameron refused. Irving would never agree to her going out of town without him.

Joshua gave up any hope of cementing their new relationship in the lap of the Spencer Inn's romantic paradise— until Archie sensed love in the air and whispered into Mac's ear.

With the house wrecked after the burglar's encounter with Gnarly, Mac thought it best for him, Archie, and Gnarly to check into his private suit on the top floor at the Inn. Bogie and David had taken the painting and disk into evidence at the police headquarters. Meanwhile, Harry Bush was calling for local federal officers to ensure nothing happened to the disk.

While their owners were taking care of business, Gnarly and Irving were having a loud debate about who ruled. Dogs or Cats? Judging by his whines and yelps, Gnarly was losing.

"Mac, have you forgotten what happened last time?" Jeff pleaded with him. "You promised me. And now you have friends checking in with a skunk? What do you think we're running here? A zoo?"

"That's not a skunk," Mac said. "It's a cat. And we couldn't leave Gnarly home alone."

"Sure," Jeff said, "But there's a very nice kennel —"

From where she was collecting the key cards for the suite, Archie shot a glance over her shoulder at the manager. Her eyebrows disappeared up into her bangs. Gnarly lowered his head like a bull preparing to charge a fighter.

Mac said, "Jeff, I assure you, I would never have brought Gnarly back to the Inn if I didn't have a very good reason for doing so."

"And what reason is that?"

"Because I said so." Archie led Gnarly to the elevator to take them up to penthouse.

"That's a good reason." Jeff turned on his heels to hurry back to his office.

Cameron laid her hand on Mac's arm. "Thank you for allowing Irving to stay here. I promise he won't be any trouble."

"No problem." Mac scratched Irving behind the ears.

Joshua offered. "Would you like to meet for a drink and do some more brainstorming? Now that the FBI has intercepted the data that the Ramsays stole, I can tell you right now that solving their murders aren't even on their radar."

"I know that," Mac said. "Have you and Cameron had dinner yet?" By the expressions on their faces, Mac saw that they'd been so wrapped up in the case that they'd forgotten about eating.

Like minds think—and don't eat—alike.

"I need to take Irving upstairs." Cameron gave Joshua a quick kiss on the lips before boarding the elevator to go upstairs to their room. "I'll meet you down here as soon as I freshen up."

The relief on Joshua's face when she left perplexed Mac. "Is she—"

"I have no idea," Joshua said. "I could use a drink. What about you?"

Mac gestured for him to follow him into the restaurant. "The bar is always open."

On the way across the lobby, Joshua asked, "Do you believe it's possible for men our age to fall in love at first sight?"

"Yep," Mac said. "It happened to me."

"My grandmother used to tell me that there was no such thing as love at first sight," Joshua said, "only lust."

Mac stopped with his hand on the door leading into the restaurant. "Are you married?"

"No."

"Is she?"

"No."

"Is she a killer, drug dealer, terrorist, or lush?"

"She doesn't smoke, drink, or do drugs," Joshua said. "But she does have a borderline addiction to junk food, which I have, too."

"What's your problem?"

"Her cat's crazy."

"I'm not the guy to talk to about that," Mac replied. "You met Gnarly." He squinted at him. "What's your real problem?"

"I have five kids that I'm going to have to explain my new friend to."

Mac looked him up and down. "Are your kids at home?"

"Only one."

"Then they're out on their own, living their own lives," Mac said. "Why can't you?"

Joshua nodded his head. "You're right."

"Of course, I am. I'm Mickey Forsythe. I'm never wrong." Mac led him inside.

Across the restaurant, Mac spied Neal Hathaway at a corner table filled with what appeared to be his people. Executive assistant Susan Dulin sat on his left side. Daughter-in-law Rachel was on his right with Scott Hathaway next to her.

Seeming to mentally block everyone out, Rachel was texting on her cell phone.

The Kaplans had seats on the other side of the table. Unhappy with the attention that her husband was paying to Susan Dulin, Nancy kept talking into Peyton's ear in a low voice. The harder he tried to ignore her, the more determined she was to capture his attention.

There was one empty chair next to Susan Dulin.

"Speak of the devil." Mac said while they followed the host to the owner's private table on the other side of the restaurant.

"I wonder which one of them leaked the discovery of Ilysa Ramsay's painting to the media?" Mac asked him after they were seated. He pointed out each member of Hathaway's party.

"Why do you think the leak was one of them? It could have been someone who worked for you."

"No one from the police department would have leaked it. Other than David, Bogie, and their crew; Archie and I were the only other ones who knew." Mac gestured in the direction of the table. "That only leaves Neal Hathaway and his entourage. One of them leaked it to the media, and I'm curious about why."

"Why are we always so suspicious?" Joshua craned his neck to see across the restaurant.

"That's what makes us such good cops."

160

Peyton Kaplan broke away from the crowd to saunter into the lounge.

Nancy paused in monitoring her husband's attention to greet a slender man with dark hair who came hurrying in from the Inn's lobby. His suit looked disheveled. When he got to the table, Nancy rose to greet him with a hug and a kiss on the cheek.

"Who's that?" Joshua asked.

"I have no idea. He's new." Mac nodded a thank you to the server for filling their water glasses. "What do you drink?" he asked Joshua.

"Scotch on the rocks." When he saw Cameron come in with Archie, he murmured to the server. "Make it a double."

"I think the man is nervous," Mac said in a low voice.

"I have reason to be." Joshua turned and flashed a smile up at Cameron when she and Archie arrived at their table. "How's Irving?"

"He scared a couple in the hall to death," Cameron said.

Joshua was nodding his head. "Irving gets screamed at alot."

Cameron smiled at him. "You didn't scream at him."

"Not on the outside." He smiled at her. "On the inside, I screamed like a little girl."

Uttering a loud noise of disgust, Rachel slammed her phone down on the tabletop. "Son of a bitch."

"Lower your voice," Scott ordered her.

Ignoring him, she shrieked, "That bastard just—"

"What bastard?" he asked her.

"What do you care?" Shrugging, she texted away on the phone.

"If I were you, I'd toss that thing into the lake," Neal said to his son.

"I do care," Scott told her in a gentle tone. "Who texted what to you?"

Those at Mac's table were craning their necks for the answer when David startled them by asking, "Is this a private party?"

Before Mac could answer, the host ordered two more chairs to be brought to their table for the newcomers. "Is the painting and chip safe?"

"That Harry dude isn't taking chances," Bogie said. "Before we left, the feds were setting up shop for until Bush gets a court order to take the chip into custody and transport it to Washington. We got four of our guys and two feds, not to mention Kenny and Harry. The chief and I had to leave, because in that small police department there wasn't any more room to sit down."

Joshua predicted, "They'll have their court order before morning."

"Which is fine with me," David said after ordering his drink. "This is my jurisdiction and, as long as it's here, it's going to be safe. Once the feds take it away, and it's no longer my responsibility, then I'll sleep better—which is why we're here."

Bogie said, "The chief and I aren't sleeping until we catch this guy. We assumed you'd all be in the same boat. So, as long as Mac's buying, let's get some chow and figure out who our killer is."

Cameron cocked her head in the direction of Neal Hathaway's table. "The killer has to be sitting over there. Give us a rundown of the players."

Mac asked, "The guy in the suit just came in. I don't know him."

The server arrived with a tray filled with drinks. While she was serving the drinks around the table, Mac asked about the man in the suit at the Hathaway table. "Oh, when he's in town, he's a regular here. His name is George Scales. Mr. Hathaway's attorney."

"Scales?" Joshua asked.

"Does he by any chance drive a black Jag?" Cameron asked the server.

Picking up her empty tray, she shrugged. "You can check at the front desk. They'll know."

Joshua told them, "That black Jag leaving the airport hangar after Bixby was killed had personalized plates. They read SCALES."

"Sounds like you need to have a discussion with Hathaway's attorney," David said.

"Ilysa put Scales in the painting," Mac said. "He looks different."

Archie nodded her head in agreement. "Because he had a facelift and nose job."

"Really? How can you tell?" Bogie asked.

Cameron agreed with Archie. "That is not the nose God gave him. It's a nice nose, but it doesn't go with his face. Yet again, boys and girls, we have a perfect example of God knowing what's best to put on your face. Instead of spending whatever Mr. Scales had to have paid for that thing, he should have stuck with what God gave him for free."

"Maybe he had to change his appearance because he didn't want to be recognized," Joshua suggested. "Maybe his picture ended up out there someplace he didn't want it to be."

"Like a famous painting," David said.

"Well," Mac said, "Hathaway called his attorney this morning about the shakedown. He and Kaplan were supposed to take care of it."

Archie said, "Scales could have set up a meeting with your boss at the hangar, and then someone killed her before he got there."

"Why are you protecting your rich friend?" Cameron asked.

"He's not my rich friend," Archie said. "You've never met Neal Hathaway. I have. He's a caring, compassionate man. When he finds out what Ilysa was doing, he'll be devastated. He really did love her."

In a soft voice, David agreed. "Yes, he did. Her murder broke him." He took a sip of his drink.

Mac said, "When you're out there on the streets like Cameron and I have been, you meet so many of the rich and powerful, who are so arrogant about proving that they're different from the rest of us, that you start to believe it—and not in a good way." He looked over at Cameron. "It can create preconceived notions about all of them."

Cameron held up her hands in surrender. "Okay. I'll open my mind. Convince me Hathaway didn't do it." She turned to Bogie. "Tell me about your murder. Who are the players, and where was each of them at the time the second Ilysa Ramsay was murdered?"

They paused to glance across the room when Rachel erupted with another shriek at something she had read on her cell phone.

Her dismay made for entertainment while each of them placed their dinner orders with the server. Afterwards, Bogie gave them a run down.

"Rachel met Scott Hathaway ten years ago when she interviewed Neal on her show *Good Morning, Pittsburgh.* She was the host of the morning show with WPXI-TV for three years until she got married. Now she's a rich man's wife and very active in the party scene."

"Where was she at the time of the murder?" Joshua asked.

"The murder happened Monday morning between twelve and one. All of our suspects claim to have been in bed asleep. Scott was in Europe. Rachel was sleeping alone. The Kaplans were up here at the Inn. They only alibi each other."

Joshua asked, "The assistant?"

"Guest room at the estate," Bogie said.

"Someone's lying," Mac said. "Someone wasn't asleep. Someone was awake and committing murder."

Abruptly, Rachel slammed her hand down on the table. After bursting into tears, she ran from the restaurant.

Cameron grinned across the table at Archie. "There comes a time in every cold case where loyalties shift. That's when the truth comes out. Now might be a time for that to happen." She picked up her handbag. "Do you feel like powdering your nose?"

"As a matter of fact, I do." Archie picked up her purse. "Excuse us, gentlemen."

ভ ঙ ও ঙ

"Bastard!"

Archie and Cameron had to stand back to let a group of women rush out to escape the wrath of Rachel Hathaway, who was acting out her fury by hurling the fresh flowers and vase, towels, and anything else that she could get her hands to throw across the room.

Calling out for security, the wash room attendant ran across the lobby, while Cameron went in. When she saw the extent of Rachel's fury, Archie took cover behind the detective.

Her hands on her hips, Cameron watched Rachel while she screamed, jumped up and down, and kicked and punched at everything in sight. The detective's expression was that of a mother watching her spoiled child throwing a tantrum.

Rachel was in the midst of yanking every warm folded-up towel off the table when the restroom door opened a crack. "Do you need help in there?"

Cameron called back over her shoulder. "We've got it covered. Thank you."

The door shut again.

"Feeling better?" Cameron asked in a calm tone when Rachel stopped to catch her breath.

"No!" She let out a wrenching sob and looked in the mirror. Displeased with what she saw, she rinsed her face and reached for a towel only to find them scattered on the floor. "Where's a towel? Why don't they have any stinking towels in here?"

With a calm demeanor, Cameron retrieved a towel from the floor and handed it to her. "How's this tantrum working for you?"

"He totally dumped me," she sobbed. "He like totally dumped me. Me! Me! Doesn't he know who I am? Nobody's ever dumped me before. Who is he to dump me? Can't he see how hot I am? Look at me!"

After agreeing that she was a catch for any man, Cameron said, "Maybe if you weren't cheating on your husband, you wouldn't be getting dumped. Did you ever think about that?"

Rachel turned to her. Her face screwed up with disgust.

"Don't you like, promise to stop dating, like when you get married?" Cameron asked with a mocking edge to her tone. "Otherwise, it's like, not really marriage, but heavy dating with fringe benefits."

"Who are you anyway?" she demanded to know.

Archie stepped around to Rachel's other side. "She's with me."

"Oh." Realizing she didn't know Archie, Rachel asked, "Who are you?"

"I'm Mac Faraday's friend." Archie offered her hand for her to shake. When Rachel refused to extend her hand to accept the offer, she withdrew it. "Archie Monday. And this is Cameron Gates, a homicide detective. She's investigating Ilysa Ramsay's murder."

Rachel whirled around to Cameron. "Oh, really?"

"Time has a way of bringing past events into focus," Cameron said. "Maybe you can remember something about that night that you missed before."

"Do you mean like Susan Dulin?" Rachel's eyes were blazing.

"What about Susan Dulin?" Archie asked.

"Her and Peyton Kaplan. They've been off and on more than a light switch. When Ilysa was killed, they were on. The night she was killed, I saw Susan running down the path to the lake."

"About what time?" Cameron glanced over at Archie to see that she was equally doubtful.

167

"It was one o'clock," Rachel said. "I'm positive, because the grandfather clock was striking one when I came downstairs to go get a drink."

"And you saw Susan outside the house on the grounds?" Archie asked. "At one o'clock in the morning?"

Rachel insisted, "If you don't believe me, ask Greta."

"Greta," Cameron asked. "Who's Greta?"

"The Hathaway housekeeper," Archie reminded her.

"Oh, Lurch!"

"Who's Lurch?" Rachel asked.

"Never mind," the detective said. "Tell us about Susan."

"When I was in the study and I saw Susan leave, I didn't want her to see me watching her. So I turned off the light," Rachel said. "That was when Greta came in through the patio door. I thought she was a burglar and she saw me and we both screamed at each other."

Cameron asked, "What was Greta doing outside?"

"She was out skinny dipping in the lake," Rachel said. "She does that late at night when no one is around."

Archie cleared her throat before telling the detective, "A lot of folks here on the lake do that."

"Do what?"

"Go skinny dipping in the middle of the night," Archie said. "I do it myself. It's quiet and invigorating. It's almost like meditating."

"Yeah," Cameron said without humor before turning back to Rachel. "What did you and the naked housekeeper talk about after screaming at each other?"

"Nothing. We had a good laugh about scaring each other. I got my drink, and I went back to bed."

"Did you tell the police about any of this?" Cameron asked her in a harsh tone.

Rachel gazed at her. "You mean I'm supposed to tell them about getting a glass of water? They asked me if I saw anything. All I saw was Susan sneaking off to meet Peyton like she does all the time."

"Was she heading in the direction of where Ilsya Ramsay was killed," Cameron asked, "and around the same time as the murder?"

"Oh." Rachel's mouth formed an "O".

While Cameron turned away in disbelief about the witness's lack of intelligence, Archie stepped in. "Could she have been sneaking out of the studio after killing Ilsya?"

Rachel still stared at her with wide eyes. "Maybe."

"Were the lights in the studio on or off?" Archie asked her.

"On." Rachel nodded her head. "Yes, they were definitely on because when the lights to the studio are on, the outside lights are on, too. I wouldn't have been able to see her if they'd been off."

"Can you think of any reason that Susan would have to hurt Ilsya Ramsay?"

"You mean other than to get her hooks into Neal?" Rachel asked. "Nah! She's totally into Peyton."

"Where did she meet Peyton?"

"Along the lake," Rachel said. "At the park. They hook up in the back of his SUV."

"How do you know that?" Archie asked. "Did you see them?"

"No, it's where he'd meet me—when he and Susan were off." Rachel held up her cell phone. "Until now—they're on again, as he just texted me."

Cameron cocked her head at her. "Let me understand this. When Susan and Peyton Kaplan are off, you and he are on. Then when he wants Susan, he dumps you—"

"Which he just texted me!" she yelled.

Archie asked, "And the night Ilysa was killed, Susan and Peyton were on and having sex in the back of his car down by the lake?"

"Until he dumped her," Rachel said. "She told me about it that morning before Ilysa's body was found. She'd been pressuring him to leave Nancy, but he told her that he could never do that. He was comfortable with the lifestyle that her and her family's money provided for him. Even if he did love Susan, he could never leave his wife."

In spite of her best effort to be sympathetic, a giggle floated to the surface when Archie asked, "Are you telling us that Peyton flat out told Susan that he was dumping her because she didn't have enough money to support him in the lifestyle to which he was accustomed?"

"What did she do when he said that?" Cameron asked.

Rachel giggled. "According to what she told me, she gave him a good swift kick in the family jewels, jumped out of the car, and came back up to the house." She asked the detective, "If I shoot him there, do you think a jury would convict me?"

Cameron asked, "Why would you have an affair with a man like that?"

"Sex," Rachel gushed. "Peyton Kaplan is *unbelievable* in bed."

Chapter Ten

"One o'clock is around the time of the murder," Bogie said between bites of his steak when Mac reported what Archie and Cameron had uncovered from Rachel in the ladies restroom. "That works for me. It's closer than we've ever been before."

Mac said, "She could have been leaving the studio after killing Ilysa, before going off to meet Peyton Kaplan."

"If she's having an affair with him," David said, "the two of them could have been working together as Ilysa's accomplices."

"If that's the case," Mac asked, "why kill Ilysa, steal the painting, and not go through with the sale?"

Joshua said, "Change of heart about betraying their country. That could be her motive. To stop the sale."

Across the restaurant, they saw Susan Dulin excuse herself from the table and leave. Now Neal and Scott Hathaway were left alone to finish coffee with Nancy Kaplan and George Scales.

"I'm torn," Mac said. "I want to question George Scales about his Jaguar leaving the scene of your murder." He pointed to Joshua. "But, I also want to ask Susan Dulin about her trip across the estate at the time of the murder."

David stood up. "I'll follow Susan while you introduce your lawyer friend to Neal Hathaway's lawyer."

Bogie objected. "You're leaving me here alone."

"You're a big boy, Bogie. Finish your steak and relax." Mac led Joshua across the dining room.

Neal Hathaway looked up with a wide smile when he saw Mac approach. "I was wondering when you'd come over to say hello." He jumped to his feet and went over to clasp his hand.

After Mac introduced Joshua as a friend visiting from out of town, Neal Hathaway went around the table to introduce his son and guests.

After a few pleasantries, Mac asked George Scales, "Did you manage to take care of that matter that Mr. Hathaway told me about today?"

"What matter?" The lawyer's face grew pale.

Joshua told him, "Someone was trying to extort money from Mr. Hathaway, and you were tasked, as his lawyer, to take care of the matter. What we want to know is, did you take care of the matter, and how?"

Neal asked Mac, "What is this about? Who did you say your friend was?"

"Joshua Thornton is a prosecutor from the Pittsburgh area," Mac replied. "This afternoon, he and an investigator discovered the murder of a detective in your airplane hangar."

Joshua kept his eyes on George Scales. "On our way into the airport, we were almost run over by a black Jaguar with personalized tags that read SCALES."

Nancy clasped George's hand. "Don't say anything."

"I didn't kill her," George insisted. "Yes, I found her body; but she was already dead, and I got out of there."

Joshua asked, "What were you doing there? Don't tell us you were coming in from a flight, because no personnel were on the scene. No flights for Hathaway Industries—arriving or departing—were booked today."

Rachel, Archie, and Cameron came into the restaurant.

The men's voices rose while the conversation escalated.

"I was there to pay her off." The lawyer mopped his forehead with his napkin. "I had a hundred and fifty thousand dollars in cash in a briefcase to give her to keep her mouth shut."

Neal threw his napkin onto the table. "Why were you paying her off? We did nothing wrong. I want to know who killed Ilysa and why. By taking care of it, I meant for you to get the authorities in to nail her butt to the wall for this!"

George Scales's face was paler than it had been before. "I thought that if I paid her something that she would go away quietly, and we wouldn't have any hassle."

"I'm a big boy," Neal said. "I expected there to be a hassle in trying to find out who killed my wife. If that's what it takes, then hassle away." He slammed his fist onto the table. "Is that why it's been eight years and the police are no closer to finding out who killed my wife? Because you've been paying people off to go away and not bother me? Well, guess what? I'm bothered!"

Scott was on his feet. "Dad, I think it's time to go home."

Neal Hathaway pointed across the table in his lawyer's direction. "You're fired! Do you hear me, Scales? Whoever killed Ilysa is walking around free, because you paid everyone off to *not bother me!*"

Scott and Rachel led Neal Hathaway, who was cussing out his attorney, out of the restaurant.

Cameron said, "He certainly looks bothered now."

Joshua asked the lawyer, "What are you afraid of?"

"Nothing." George Scales rose to his feet. He turned to come face to face with Cameron.

"I think that pay off was to protect you," the detective said.

Nancy took him by the arm. "If you want to ask any more questions, call our lawyer."

Cameron asked, "Do you two both have the same lawyer?"

Nancy shot a glare at her before dragging Scales out of the restaurant.

附 ᔓ ᖇ ᔑ

David had trailed Susan Dulin into the rose garden maze. A romantic, softly-lit, floral garden, it was a favorite spot for couples to have privacy late at night.

Mac and Archie waited for Susan and Peyton to be in the throes of a passionate embrace before interrupting them.

"Fancy meeting you here," Mac plopped down on the stone bench next to Susan Dulin, who quickly covered up her blouse that had become unbuttoned.

"Can't you see we want to be alone?" Peyton glared up at Archie, who blocked his path of escape when he tried to slip away. His glare deepened when he turned to see David blocking the only other escape route.

"You lied to us," David said. "The night Ilysa Ramsay was murdered, you both stated that you were asleep. You, Kaplan, told us you were up here at the Inn with your wife. You, Dulin, told us you were asleep in your room. Now, we find out that you both were lying and you, Dulin, actually went for a jog across the estate at the time of the murder—"

"I left my room after one o'clock," she said. "It was *after* the murder. I was asleep until twelve-thirty."

Peyton laughed, "Do you actually think we did it? Well, we do have alibis. Better than the one we gave you before. We were with each other until close to four in the morning."

"But you got together around the time of the murder," Mac said. "Susan, you were seen right there at the studio."

"Who told you that?" She scoffed. "Let me guess? Rachel?"

Peyton asked, "Why would Susan kill Ilysa?"

"You tell us," David challenged him. "Maybe it has something to do with that little nestegg you have in the Cayman Islands."

Susan whirled around to face Peyton. "You have a nestegg in the Cayman Islands!"

"A small nestegg." Peyton press his finger and thumb together to indicate a small amount.

Doubting him, Susan looked up at David, who shook his head. She sucked in a deep breath and slapped Peyton across the face. "All these years you've been telling me that you can't leave your wife because you can't live without her money when you've been socking it away and not telling me!" She slapped him again. "You dirty rotten liar!"

When she threw her arm back to hit him again, Mac grabbed it. "I think you've punished him enough."

"No, I haven't." She tried to pull her arm free, but Mac had a firm hold on it.

Mac asked Peyton, "Where did that money come from?"

"An inheritance," he said.

"He's lying," Susan told them. "No one in his family likes him enough to want to leave him anything."

"Oh, yeah?" Peyton replied. "Fat lot you know. This inheritance came from a distant cousin who didn't know me very well. So there!" He stuck his tongue out at her.

With a *humph*, she turned her head away.

David asked her, "Was Peyton already waiting at the park when you went to meet him?"

She rolled her eyes. "Yes, he was already there waiting for me. Creep."

"How would you describe him?" Mac asked her.

"What do you mean?"

"What was his mood? Was he agitated? Excited?"

"He was horny—like always."

Archie clarified. "He was excited."

Susan said, "I did not kill Ilysa. Why would I? So I went pass her studio around the time of the murder?"

"If you didn't do it," Mac said, "you may have seen who did."

"All I saw was Greta, naked, walking up the path from the lake. She'd been swimming."

"Swimming? Naked?" Mac asked. "At one o'clock in the morning?"

Archie whispered to him, "It's not unusual. I go skinny dipping in the lake late at night sometimes."

Peyton's eyes brightened. "Do you?"

"I also carry a pink handgun that I use to shoot peepers."

Mac asked them, "Now that we're remembering what we should have told the police back years ago, can either of you think of anyone, besides Victor Gruskonov, who had a reason to hurt Ilysa?"

They glanced at each other before looking back at them and shrugging.

Mac asked Susan, "How about on the way back from the park? What happened after you left Peyton?"

"It was four o'clock. I jogged back up the path along the lake to the mansion."

"Were the lights on or off in the art studio?" Mac asked her. "Off."

Mac asked, "Are you sure?"

"Positive."

"How about when you left to go meet Peyton … at one o'clock?"

"Off."

"Both times?"

The repeated question made her glare and bite off both words in her answer. "I'm positive."

"Okay." Mac stood up. "You can go back to what you were doing."

With a sneer at Peyton, she replied, "Don't even think about it."

CB ƏD CR ƏD

Did I used to be this nervous?

While waiting for Cameron to come out of the bathroom, Joshua stroked Irving, who had taken a strong liking to him. In the past, he had been confident and in charge of every situation. If anything, the woman was nervous.

Now, that seemed so long ago. It was back when he was the high school football hero, and then the Naval Academy cadet. It was before marriage and children, and settling back into the sedate life of a single father with grown children.

A lifetime ago.

His reflection in the hotel mirror revealed that he was no longer the dashing football hero or Naval officer.

Now he was a middle-aged man ... with the gray to prove it.

It seemed to be overnight that Joshua's hair had turned from auburn to silver. With humor, he noted that it was about the time that his two oldest sons left home for college.

When his barber, Sam, suggested coloring it, Joshua objected. "I've earned every one of these gray hairs." Calling it his badge of maturity, he was so proud of his silver locks that he even let his hair grow out to the top of his shirt collar into what he saw as a silver mane.

Now, waiting for Cameron to join him for their first night alone, he wondered at his reflection in the mirror. *What's going through her mind when she looks at me? Does she see a man as old as my children seem to think I am?*

Little did he know that a similar conversation was going on in the bathroom.

03 80 03 80

Cameron was relieved to find that Irving actually liked Joshua. He didn't become spastic about him like other men she had dated. Maybe that was why Irving liked him.

No one likes being screamed at. It isn't Irving's fault that he looks like a skunk.

Since the road trip was last minute, all Cameron had time to pack was an old tiger-striped nightie. It wasn't until she looked at her reflection in the mirror that she recalled her reason for buying it.

It was for her honeymoon.

A wave of guilt washed over her.

How could I have forgotten a thing like that?

She stripped the nightie off and tossed it to the floor.

Now what?

Swallowing her guilt, she brushed her hair while thinking back over the years. Her new husband dying months after the wedding; her spiraling out of control while trying to wash away the pain with alcohol; and crashing at rock bottom emotionally, as well as professionally. With nothing left, she quit everything and walked away. There was nothing left to do but reflect, regroup, and reassemble her life and priorities.

Getting back to what was important.

She washed her face. When she stood up and looked at her reflection, she smiled at what she saw.

It's not about a nightie. It's not about looking perfectly sexy. It's not about sex with a silver fox. It's about more than that. He was more important to her than a night of wild sexual abandon. She knew that when he first laughed at her jokes.

Joshua Thornton is a keeper.

She threw her grass stained shirt on over her panties and stepped out of the bathroom. "Are you ready?"

She was relieved to see that he had taken off at least his shirt. He patted the pillow on the other side of the bed. "I don't know if Irving is. He seems to think this is his spot."

Cameron slipped in under the covers. She noticed what appeared to be a shadow cross his face. "What's wrong?"

He directed his attention to Irving, who pressed his head against his hand to beg for more petting. "I think you should know something."

"You've got a girlfriend." She held her breath.

"No, far from that."

"A boyfriend?"

He snapped his head up to look at her. "I have five kids."

"I knew that," she replied. "Do you have a boyfriend?"

"No, I don't have a boyfriend."

"Then what?" Now she was really worried.

"I haven't had a serious relationship since my wife died." Joshua looked over at her. "Every time I've gotten close, I've been scared off."

She reached over to stroke his face. "Guilt."

"Yeah. A lot of guilt." He caressed her face. "When I started this vacation, ending up here with someone like you was the last place I expected to be."

"Is that good or bad?" Gazing into his clear blue eyes, she moved over closer to him.

"We'll let you be the judge of that."

Seeming to sense he was being squeezed out, Irving jumped off the bed and landed over on the dresser.

She reached under the covers to place her hand on his hip and was delighted to find that her fingers stroked bare flesh. *So far, so good.* She sat up and pulled her shirt off over her head. "What do you say we make this a vacation to write home about?"

"Not to my family." He pulled her down to kiss him.

ભ ૭ ૪ ૭

In the private penthouse suite up on the top floor of the Spencer Inn, room service had delivered champagne and strawberries while they were out. Candles and the see-through fireplace bathed the suite in a soft glow.

Clad in her red silk robe, Archie waited next to the table set for two for Mac to come out of the bathroom. "I wondered when you were going to get up the nerve to come out. Dessert is waiting." With that, she dropped the robe.

He wrapped his arms around her. "I guess I better dig in before it gets cold."

They embraced. With each kiss their passion grew until he took her into his arms and lifted her up.

The bedroom being further away than he wanted to go, he carried her to the sofa. Together, they dropped onto the cushions.

Startled out of a deep sleep, Gnarly's yelp broke the moment. All three bodies tumbled onto the floor in a mass of arms, legs, fur, and paws.

"Gnarly," Mac said to the dog draped across his chest, "I'm going to kill you."

Chapter Eleven

"We put that crime scene tape up for a reason," Mac heard David call to him from the dock.

If Mac had caught a private citizen inside a burnt-out van surrounded by crime scene tape when he'd been a detective, he wouldn't have been as nice as David. Even if it was Mac's dock and his speed boat under the thief's van, he was supposed to wait for the police department to clear the scene before climbing inside.

"Are you through in the house?" Mac resumed his search. The evidence gloves felt like a favorite pair of jeans he liked wearing when he wanted to be comfortable. The flashlight he used to search the charred interior felt like a partner he never should have let go.

"It's clear. Now your contractor can repair the damage from Gnarly's audition for the lead beast in a horror movie." David stepped back to avoid getting splashed when Gnarly dove in after a flock of ducks taunting him from the water.

Gnarly was having a grand time playing a dog-duck version of tag. He would chase the ducks roosting around the dock out into the deep water of the lake, only to have them turn around and chase him back to shore. Then, after reaching his limit of being taunted by the water fowl, he would dive back into the water to chase them out again.

"Did you get anything on the gun that Gnarly found?"

"It was stolen during a burglary in New York," David said. "The guy's a pro, Mac. We got his ID. Felix Grant aka Felix the Cat Burglar."

"Cat?" Mac called out from inside the van. "No wonder Gnarly took him out the way he did."

"He's wanted in three states. The police in Massachusetts, New York, and Virginia are fighting over him for charges of breaking and entering, and burglary."

That was enough to make Mac stick his head out the van's window. "What was he doing here in Spencer?"

"Someone hired him. Like I said, he's a pro. He's already lawyered up." David grinned. "He's a real character. He talks about himself in third person. 'Felix the Cat is the best, and you never would have caught Felix the Cat if it hadn't been for that werewolf.'"

"I always said Gnarly was a beast."

The German Shepherd ran back up onto the bank via the boat launch to shake the water out of his fur. David stepped back to once again avoid the spraying water.

"Do you have your cell phone?" Mac asked.

"Where's yours?"

"I left it in my car. I'll give it back."

David removed his phone from his utility belt.

Mac took a burnt up smart phone from an evidence bag. "I found this under the front seat of the van." He removed the cover to reveal the smart chip inside, which he slipped into David's cell phone. "See if you can bring up his call log to see who Felix the Cat has been talking to."

After pressing a few buttons, David brought the phone to his ear and smiled when he made a connection. "Hey, I got your merchandise.…The dog gave me some issues, but I took care of him."

When Gnarly barked as if to protest the police chief's lie, David turned his head away while Mac shushed him.

"Do you have my money?" David went on to set up the appointment before hanging up. "Good work, Faraday. The drop is one o'clock this afternoon at a lakeside café in McHenry." He removed the chip and placed it into the evidence bag along with the phone. "Now get out of that van before you get hurt and sue the department."

"Did you recognize the voice of the perp?" Mac asked while steadying himself as he climbed onto the dock.

"Can't tell."

With the clear summer day, there were a number of jet skis out racing about on the lake not far from shore. David sat down on the bench at the end of the dock. Gnarly trotted up to rest his wet head in his lap. In silence, he stroked the dog's head without noticing that his wet fur was leaving a water mark on his pant leg that would make it appear as if he had peed his pants.

"I've been thinking about Hathaway," David said.

"Hathaway? What about him?"

"You weren't there when Bogie and I arrived at the scene of Ilysa's murder," David said. "Detective Gates doesn't believe that a man can't tell that his wife was replaced with a duplicate, but this man really loved her. It was heartbreaking to see. When he finds out that his wife had used him to steal the access codes for his satellites to sell to terrorists—I can't bear the thought."

"I can't see how we can't tell him."

Staring out at the water, David was silent. Finally, he said in a soft voice, "I want to be the one to do it." He looked over at Mac. "But first, I want to find out who killed her and why." He continued staring out at the water while stroking Gnarly's head. "That will make it easier for him if he has more answers."

Mac clasped his shoulder. "We'll catch this guy."

David stopped petting Gnarly. "I know."

 CB   ED   CA   ED

"You're staring," David told Mac, who was gazing straight ahead from the driver's seat of his SUV.

"It's a stake out. I'm supposed to stare."

"But the perp is meeting my officer down there." David pointed at the lakeside café down the hill from where they had parked on John Young Parkway. "You're so spaced out that our guy could walk right in front of us with the painting and you wouldn't notice."

After learning that Felix's client didn't know what he looked like, one of Spencer's slightly built officers posed as him at the café in McHenry. While Spencer's police officers waited on one side of the restaurant, Joshua and Cameron had parked on the far side, in case the drop happened there.

"You're too far away," David argued when Mac parked at the end of the lot reserved for patrons of the lakeside diners and water sports vendors. A dirt path led down to the water where the exchange was scheduled to take place.

"If we park along the road the perp will see us," Mac said.

"If he rabbits, we'll be useless in catching him."

"I've done this before," Mac said. "Wait and learn." But, instead of watching for their suspect, he was thinking about Archie and her nightly escapes from his bed. "How do you know if you snore?"

"Someone tells you…the announcement is usually preceded by a sharp jab to the ribs."

"Christine would have told me if I snored," Mac said more to himself than David. "She wouldn't have been nice about it either."

One of David's eyebrows arched, while a corner of his mouth curled. "Is something going on between you and Archie?"

"Something has been going on between me and Archie since the day I came to Spencer." He added, "No, we haven't been sleeping together that long. As a matter of fact, we haven't been sleeping together at all."

David turned around to face him. "Do you mean—"

"I mean—Sure, we've been together," Mac told him. "We both wanted it to be special. I took her to Paris for Valentine's Day."

David said, "I know. I house and dog sat for you. While you were gone Gnarly bellied into the Schweitzer house and stole Katherine's blue marquis diamond from where she had left it on her dresser. We turned Spencer upside down for five days before you told me to look under your bed."

"I still think you should have cuffed Gnarly, instead of having Bogie slip it into her purse while you were interviewing her," said Mac. "I never would have figured you to be one to take part in a police cover up."

"How do you explain to the media that the great jewel thief that everyone has been looking for, that stole a half-a-million dollar diamond, was really a klepto German Shepherd?" David raised a shoulder. "Katherine had no problem believing that she'd misplaced it. No harm, no foul."

"Until Gnarly's next caper."

"That's not my problem. He's your dog," David reminded him. "Tell me about you and Archie."

"Things are great." Mac rubbed away a smudge on the windshield.

"Then why the staring?"

Mac turned to him. "She won't sleep with me." He hated the wounded sound that had crept into his tone.

The police chief laughed. "That's something else that's not my problem."

Frustrated, Mac said, "No, I mean we have a great relationship. We're very compatible in that way."

David was still laughing.

"I mean," he said forcibly, "she won't spend the night with me in my bed. As soon as I'm asleep, she goes back to the cottage. She says it's because she can only sleep in her bed. But last night, at the Inn, she went to the other bedroom as soon as I was asleep."

Even though he had stopped laughing, David was still smiling when he said, "Maybe you snore."

"My ex-wife would have told me." Mac turned his attention back to the café. "At some point, over the matter of twenty years, she would have certainly told me if I snored."

Keeping an eye on the drop site, David suggested, "Maybe you thrash around. I used to date a woman who was all over that bed during the night—kicking and hitting—and she was asleep the whole time. Sleeping with her was like wrestling an octopus."

"And you ended it," Mac noted.

David's face softened. "You're right. If you snored, or punched and kicked during the night, after being married for so long, you'd know it by now."

"Then why does Archie keep running off?"

"This is new." David was chuckling again. "A woman running off as soon as sex is over, and the man wanting her to stay and cuddle."

Mac punched the steering wheel and grumbled. "Forget I said anything. You're right. I'm being silly. I don't know why. I didn't used to be that way. But, since I met Archie, I've turned into some adolescent—"

David reached across the front of the car to grasp his wrist. Compassion seeped in to replace his amusement. "Let me explain something about us."

"Us?"

"I mean the rich."

"You're not rich," Mac reminded him. "You're an underpaid police chief in a rich town."

"But I've spent my whole life among the rich," David said. "And Archie may have been Robin's assistant, but she's spent over the last ten years living among them. I know you like to think we're no different, but in some ways we are."

Mac shook his head. "David, I've investigated more than one murder involving rich people."

"You've seen them in the midst of scandal and controversy," David pointed out. "Growing up in Spencer, going to school with their kids, playing ball with them, dating their daughters; I've seen them day by day. It's not what people see on reality TV, or on the news when one of them kills the other. I know what these people are really like."

Mac was getting impatient. "What does this have to do with Archie and me?"

"It's not unusual for couples who are intimate with each other, who have great relationship, and enjoy each other's company, to sleep in separate bedrooms," David said. "It doesn't mean they don't love each other. Among the rich, many couples, each partner has their own room or suite—even though they may have roof shattering sex with each other—and they don't cheat on each other. They just have their own space. Why? Because they can."

"I grew up where couples were together," Mac said. "They sleep together in the same bed."

"Here's something else to consider," David told him, "Archie is in her middle thirties. She's never been married. She's never had a long-term relationship—at least, as long as I've known her. She loves you, but she's used to having her own space. Man! What more do you want?"

The thought struck Mac like a bolt of lightning. "Did you ever date Archie?"

The corner of David's lip curled. "Timing never worked out."

"But you tried."

"She wasn't ready for a serious relationship," David explained. "Dad got sick and was sick a long time before he died. So, I was in no shape for a relationship. By the time things settled …" He laughed. "Dating Archie would be like dating my sister. That's what makes her the perfect woman for my brother." He turned to him. "Give her time. Things will sort themselves out. They always do."

"Never thought of that." Mac was impressed with the police chief's ability to see things as they really were.

David was perceptive beyond his years. It came from growing up in Spencer among the rich, without being one of them. It must have been like being next to the forest, while not being in it. Therefore, he was able to see the trees in the forest.

Mac said, "I hate sleeping alone."

"Which I believe is the root to why it's bothering you." David patted him on the shoulder. "Don't worry. You two will work it out." With a smirk, he said, "Geek at eleven o'clock."

Directing his attention back at the café, Mac picked out the patron, who had caught the police chief's attention. Two tables away from the officer in plain clothes, he was hard for them not to notice.

In the middle of the day, during the height of the summer season, most of the patrons were donning casual summer wear. In contrast, the man sipping hot tea and eating a scone stood out in white slacks and a bright pink shirt buttoned up to the collar and sealed with a dark pink tie. A duffel bag rested in an empty chair across from him. His appearance was made even more outlandish by his bi-color hair with dark around the sides and back, and white spikes on top. He sported a black goatee.

He took a sip of his tea before spitting it out into the cup. After letting out a gagging noise, he snapped his fingers high above his head to get the server's attention. "Excuse me," he called out in broken English with a thick European accent, "but … this tea has been … ruined."

"Ruined? How?" The server glanced around for help. Ruined tea was a new complaint.

"Tea should never … be allowed to seep for more … than five minutes." The patron stuck his pointy nose high up in the air in order to look down his snout at her. "Any longer than that and it's not…" While waving his hand in the air, he paused to search for the word. "How do you say?…Edible."

Apologizing, the server took the cup and tea pot to return them to the kitchen.

The tea man was on the move. After picking up the duffle bag, he moved to the undercover officer's table in the center of the café.

"Anything looking good today?" He gave the officer the code.

The officer said his line, "The margaritas."

Eying the tube envelope next to the officer's hand, the tea man inched his fingertips toward it. "Did you have any…How do you say? … Problems?"

"The dog."

A worried note came to his voice. "Did you to hurt him?"

"Felix the Cat is a professional." The officer repeated the thief's assertion in third person as he had done in the hospital.

The tea man reached for the tube, which the officer slid out of his reach. "After I get my money."

The tea man dropped the bag to the ground, and pushed it with his foot over to the other seat. Looking around as if to ensure that they were not being watched, the officer picked up the bag and looked inside.

"Fifty-thousand dollars. You can count it." His mustache grew wide with his smile of anticipation. He snatched the tube.

"I'll trust you." The officer stood up. "Nice doing business with you."

When the tea man removed the cap of the tube and peered inside, the police poured in from all directions. "Police! You're under arrest."

The call startled the man with the goatee, but not so much that he was willing to give up easily.

"He's going to rabbit." David grabbed the door handle. "Told you so."

Mac stopped him. "Wait for it."

Crying out, the tea man made a run for it. Knocking a server with a tray full of food out of his way, he ran for the side of the cafe and took the path up the hill toward the parking lot. He headed straight for Mac's SUV. After cresting the hill, he ran for the lot, and then darted alongside the car—only to slam into the driver's side door that Mac kicked open.

The force of the door caused him to fall backwards and roll head over heels, with the tube toppling alongside him, back down the hill to the officers below.

"Not bad," David said. "You caught him without breaking a sweat."

Mac closed the door and sat back in his seat. "And you didn't want to park up here."

❧ ❧ ❧ ❧

On the other side of the café, Joshua and Cameron watched the police officers chase after the man with the spiked hair. While the mob ran in one direction, they watched a man with dark hair get up from where he had been watching on a bench along the lakeshore. He quickened his pace toward the Jaguar parked next to them.

He was still watching to make sure no one had spotted him when he reached for the door handle.

Joshua gripped his wrist. "So we meet again, Mr. Scales."

"Thornton." He turned to find Cameron flanking him. "I was out enjoying the beautiful summer weather."

"How long do you think the courier you hired will keep quiet under questioning?" Cameron asked him.

"I don't know what you're talking about."

Joshua said, "Things will go better for you if you come clean."

"I've done nothing wrong."

"Then why are you paying people off and trying to buy stolen paintings?" Joshua asked.

Scales stuttered. "I-I have a client. Anonymous."

"Do you mean Nancy Kaplan?"

"I'm not saying a word—"

"I know, I know," Cameron said. "Until you talk to your lawyer."

"Oh, Scales…"

George Scales whirled around to find that the police cruiser had pulled up behind them. Bogie was at the steering wheel. David held the back door open and the tea man was nodding his head at the lawyer. "That's him! That's the guy that offered me five thousand dollars to pick up his package for him." The European accent had disappeared.

David gestured for Scales to get in. "Care to join us?"

George Scales whipped out his cell phone. "I'm calling my lawyer."

Cameron told him, "Good help is so hard to find."

Chapter Twelve

Under an arrogant exterior, George Scales's nervousness showed in the tapping of his heels in the interrogation room.

In the squad room, Cameron and Bogie were racing to get the results of a background check on the lawyer, who had a long list of high profile clients, most of whom were government defense contractors.

Joshua asked Cameron, "Have you gotten any word from your people in Pittsburgh about Scales being at the scene when Bixby was killed?"

"We have the call from his cell phone to her throw away phone. But there was a call she received about ten minutes before that from another throw away phone. That call lasted about three minutes.

"That could be Kaplan," Mac said from where he was sitting next to Officer Foster's desk. "Hathaway told us that he called

Kaplan and his lawyer to take care of it. If Scales was working on his own, and he didn't kill Bixby, then that leaves Kaplan… or someone Kaplan sent."

"Like his wife," Joshua said, "She seemed awfully chummy with Scales last night."

Cameron recalled, "She was the one that ordered him not to say anything—maybe she had her own reasons."

"We have another off-shore account," Bogie announced.

They crowded around the deputy chief's chair to see the listing on his computer screen.

"Scales has over ten million dollars in the Cayman Islands," Bogie said. "I also took a look at Peyton Kaplan's account. That has only two million dollars."

Cameron laughed. "*Only* two million?"

"I wonder how much classified information is going for?" Bogie asked.

Joshua leaned in to look at the computer screen. "Can you find out whose account that money came out of?"

"Let me do some digging." Bogie bent over the keyboard to peck at the keys.

David recalled, "Peyton claims his money was inherited, and he was hiding it from his wife."

"Hell of a guy," Cameron muttered. "I don't like him."

Bogie yelled, "Found it. In both accounts, the money has been transferred from an online investment company. There have been transfers as recent as three days ago. The name on the account is Ann Scales, who resides at 1313 Penn Way in Pittsburgh."

"Wait a minute. I know that address." Cameron was inputting the address into her smart phone while Bogie read it off. She smirked. "It's a nursing home. How much do you want to bet Ann Scales is George's mother?"

"They're laundering the money they're making selling defense secrets through Scales's mother," Joshua said. "I wonder how many defense secrets they've sold to terrorists throughout the years?"

David said, "What do you say we go find out, Bogie?"

"Can I play the bad cop?" Bogie punched his hand with his fist. "I don't like traitors."

David patted him on the arm. "You can be whoever you want to be, big guy."

Ↄ ⁊ ↅ ⁊

"So, Scales," David said when he came into the interrogation room. "You like paintings." He tossed the Ramsay case file onto table.

With a hard expression on his face, Bogie struck an intimidating figure while standing in front of the door with his arms folded across his broad chest. David swung around the chair on the opposite side of the table from Scales and straddled the back. The police chief shot the suspect a boyish grin.

They came across as the classic bad cop-good cop.

George eyed the folder. "Of course, I like paintings."

"Enough to kill for them?" David fingered the folder that rested on the table between them.

"I told you already," Scales said. "I have a client who happens to be a big Ilysa Ramsay fan. I thought this was a legitimate pur—" His eyes grew wide as they darted from Bogie's scowl to David's pleasant expression.

"If you thought it was so legit why did you hire someone to pick it up for you while you watched from ten yards away?" Chuckling, David glanced up at Bogie. The corner of the big cop's lip curled to allow a low growl to seep from his massive chest.

As if ignoring Bogie would make him disappear, George Scales forced himself to focus on David. "My client really wanted this painting. Book me for conspiracy to commit burglary, and I'll be on my way."

"Ah, I'd really like to do that." David shook his head while thumbing the edges of the case file without actually opening it. "But we can't let you go anywhere. This isn't a simple case of burglary. You're looking at murder, my man."

George's eyes were focused on the folder. "No one was killed in that break-in."

"Except Mac Faraday's new boat," Bogie said in a deep loud voice. "He was taking me out on it tomorrow, and now I can't go."

"I'll buy him a new one." His voice went up so high that it squeaked. "I'll have it delivered ASAP. I'll get him a bigger one. One more your size."

"What are you going to buy it with?" David asked, "The ten mil you have in the Cayman Islands?"

At that, Scales face became paler.

David grinned up at Bogie.

In the interrogation room, Mac chuckled along with them. "We have him."

"That's what you're afraid of people finding out," David said. "That's why you were so anxious to pay off Lieutenant Bixby to allow the Ramsay case to go cold. You couldn't afford to have the authorities poking around too much."

"Are you talking about that woman that tried to shake us down about Ilysa's murder? I told you and that woman detective, she was already dead when I got there."

"Why did you go there?" David asked.

"Because that was where she told me to meet her and take one hundred and fifty thousand dollars."

"How did you set up the meeting?"

Scales rolled his eyes. "Hathaway called me a little after nine o'clock yesterday morning at my office in Pittsburgh. He said one of your people was trying to shake him down by claiming that she had information that would hurt him or make him look guilty of Ilysa's murder. He told Kaplan to take care of it—"

"Which meant what?" Bogie asked.

Scales sucked in a deep breath. "You met Hathaway. He's the straightest of straight arrows. He wanted this blackmailer caught and locked up—after she told us who killed Ilysa."

David said, "That was the last thing you wanted, because it might come out that you've been stealing government secrets from your clients and selling them to our enemies."

"You have no proof of that."

"Are you sure about that?" David leaned toward him and lowered his voice. "What if I told you that we have proof that you were in Deep Creek Lake when Ilysa Ramsay was murdered?"

Scales's eyes narrowed.

In the observation room, Cameron asked Mac, "Do we have proof of that?"

"We can get it."

Joshua said, "As slow as he's answering, I think David's bluff worked. He's got to think about how best to answer. Continue denying any wrongdoing, or come clean and make a deal."

"I did not kill Ilysa Ramsay," Scales said. "Her team was supposed to be the best. They were highly recommended. But as soon as she married Hathaway everything went haywire. First of all, she disappeared and no one knew where she was. She was to meet Hathaway for a rocket launching in Arizona, but something happened and she didn't show up. Hathaway was frantic."

David asked, "Was that in June 2003?"

"It was right after they were married." Scales shrugged. "Maybe. Then she showed up. I forget what she said had happened. But weeks of work went to pot. Then, Hathaway was working on this huge new system and I got a lot of interest in that. But then, things went real bad."

"I know how that can be," David said like they were two drinking buddies at the bar. "How bad did it get?"

"The worst," George said. "That little bitch...She kept nosing around and asking questions. Next thing I know, she has my account records and a recording of me and Kaplan—Bitch!"

George dropped back in his seat and clinched his jaw.

"What type of recording?" When he received no answer, David shrugged his shoulders. "We found out about your bank account. The money is being transferred from your mother's account. Now, considering that she's a nursing home resident, we know the money is being laundered through her account. We're going to find out, Scales. So you might as well fess up." He leaned across the table and asked in a low voice, "Who have you been selling our secrets to?"

"It's not from selling secrets," George smirked.

In the observation room, Joshua's eyes lit up. "Kaplan is on the board. Scales has all these executive clients—It's insider trading. They're doing inside trading under Scales's mother's name."

It was as if David heard him on the other side of the two-way mirror. "The money was transferred into your account from an online investment firm. You've been playing the stock market in your mother's name using inside information that you've been collecting from your clients on the boards of defense companies."

George Scales's eyes narrowed to slits.

"Peyton Kaplan's account is his cut from money that you made based on information he gave you." David chuckled. "Ilysa Ramsay found out and blackmailed you two."

"Kaplan never knew that I had hired Gruskonov and his team," Scales said. "He thought I had gotten mixed up in it because of the insider trading that Ilysa nailed us on. I figured she would just play this game until she got the information for me to sell, but then—" He slammed his hand down on the table and glared at the police chief. "The little bitch turned on us."

"How did she turn on you?" David asked. "Was she holding out for a bigger cut?"

"Worse than that," Scales said. "She recorded everything. She was going to turn Kaplan and me in for the theft and the insider trading."

"Guess that goes to show you," David said, "there's no loyalty among thieves."

Batting his eyelashes, Scales said in a mocking tone, "She was in love." He turned serious. "This was her last job for

Gruskonov. She didn't want to do it, but Gruskonov forced her hand, and then she turned the tables on us. As soon as it was over, we were to resign and go away quietly, or go to jail."

"Sounds like a good reason for killing her to me," Bogie said. "Don't you think so, Chief?"

"I can see why you'd be furious," David said. "It must have been some fight you had with her for messing up your plans."

"No!" Scales's eyes became wide. "She had no idea she was working for me. That was part of the set up. The only one who knew the players was Victor Gruskonov—who disappeared off the face of the earth. I assumed he took the merchandise. But then, when Nancy told me that Faraday had the painting, I thought maybe—it was worth a shot to see if the merchandise was still with the painting. So, I contacted the media about it so that when the painting was stolen, you'd think it was someone else in the art world who took it—maybe even Gruskonov, who stole it in the first place."

"Actually," David said, "he was killed in a car accident the night of the pick-up. He never had a chance to get the painting."

"Then, who stole it?" Scales asked. "Did they get the merchandise?"

"Who else knew about your side business?"

Scales was silent.

"Who's your client?" David asked, "Nancy Kaplan? Her husband was alibiing someone else at the time—"

"You mean Susan Dulin," Scales said.

"Peyton Kaplan was with Susan Dulin. And you were with—"

"Okay, I was in Deep Creek Lake," Scales confessed. "I was staying in the other wing at the Spencer Inn. As soon as Peyton slipped out at midnight, after he thought Nancy was asleep, she called me. I came over and left at four o'clock, when the doorman called to tell me that Peyton was back."

In the observation room, Cameron laughed. "What is wrong with these people? Why do they even bother getting married when they're all sleeping with other people?"

Mac assured her, "We're not all like that."

In the interrogation room, David sighed. "Does Nancy Kaplan know about your side business?"

"Why do you think I do it?" George said. "She would never leave Peyton for a poor man. I thought that as soon as I made enough to have as much money as these guys I represent, I was going to take Nancy and we were going to run off to the Cayman Islands, and I could be one of them instead of working for them."

David slapped his hand down on the case file and stood up. "Instead you're going to a federal pen and living like the traitor that you are." He told Bogie, "Lock him up."

"Gladly," the deputy chief replied.

In the interrogation room, Mac, Joshua, and Cameron turned away.

"Scales didn't kill Ilysa and he didn't steal that painting," she said. "I don't see him having the guts to kill Bixby."

"I believe I know who did," Mac said.

Chapter Thirteen

They arrived at the Hathaway estate in a convoy. Mac and Archie were in her SUV, which had Gnarly riding in the back seat; David and Bogie rode in Spencer's police cruiser; and Joshua and Cameron brought up the rear in her Pennsylvania state police cruiser.

Greta was not happy to see a crowd standing on the doorstep. "Can I help you?"

Mac asked her, "Is Susan Dulin in?"

"She's in her office in the east wing." She opened the door to let them in. "Do keep that dog on a leash."

Gnarly regarded her order with groan.

Greta led them to the back of the mansion where they went down a hallway to the right and through the kitchen, which was littered with grocery bags and boxes of food and kitchen supplies.

While he hurried behind her, Mac asked, "I understand you left something out in your statement to the police about the night of Ilysa's murder."

She didn't bother turning around. "What did I leave out?"

"About you not being asleep in your room that night."

Greta stopped so fast that Mac collided into her. She turned around. "Who told you that?"

"A witness," Mac said.

Archie added, "Two, in fact."

Greta looked at them. "Who? What did they tell you?"

"About your fondness for skinny dipping down at the lake late at night," Archie said.

A grin crossed Greta's face. "Is that all?"

David asked, "Why didn't you tell us when we asked where you'd been?"

"Susan asked me to lie," Greta said. "If she admitted to being with Mr. Kaplan, then his wife would have found out. If I said I was out swimming, you would ask me if I saw anything and if I said I saw nothing, and someone had seen Susan then—It was easier to lie. It isn't like I saw anything that could help to find Ms. Ramsay's killer." She peered at David. "Am I in trouble?"

David glanced over at Mac who was examining a box of strawberries on the kitchen counter.

"These are some enormous strawberries," Mac said. "How much do they cost?" He picked up the receipt from the kitchen counter. "Hey, Archie, do you know how to make strawberry shortcake?"

"Do you mind?" Greta grabbed the receipt from his hand. "I bought them at the farmer's market this morning. Mr. Hathaway likes his produce fresh." She shooed Gnarly down from where he was sniffing a box. "Will you get your dog out of the kitchen please? I don't want dog hair in Mr. Hathaway's dinner."

Archie pulled Gnarly down from where he was counter surfing with his front paws up on the counter.

"Another thing," Mac asked the housekeeper, "When you were swimming naked in the lake, were the lights on or off in the studio?"

Greta stared at him for a long beat before answering, "I don't remember."

"Are you sure?" Mac looked back at her. "It's important."

She shook her head. "I'm sorry. I wish I could help."

Mac told her, "It would mean so much to Mr. Hathaway if he could find out the truth about what happened to his wife. Closure in these types of things mean a lot."

"We have to talk to Ms. Dulin," Cameron reminded Mac in a sharp voice.

"Think about it," Mac told Greta.

The housekeeper gestured to the other side of the kitchen. "Their office is this way."

When they stepped down into the next room, the atmosphere took on that of an office with desks, computers, printers, and file cabinets. Susan Dulin looked up from her laptop at the group that filed in. "What is this about?"

Mac began, "You were with Peyton Kaplan in the back of his SUV at the time of Ilysa Ramsay's murder."

"I told you that last night." She sat back in her chair and interlaced her fingers across her midriff. "We can alibi each other. We were together almost all night when Ilysa was murdered. Now tell me something new."

"Mac, what are you doing here?" Neal Hathaway came out of his office with Scott and Rachel.

"We know who stole Ilysa's painting," Mac announced.

Neal followed Mac's eyes to Susan at her desk.

Rachel gasped and covered her mouth with her hand. "Susan! How could you?" When the assistant glared up at her, a wicked grin crossed Rachel's face.

"Susan?" Neal asked in a low voice. "Now you?"

Mac leaned over her desk. "When did you decide to take it?"

"You can't prove anything."

Bogie said, "The paint was still fresh when it was stolen. Will we find your fingerprints on the canvas when we dust it?"

Mac sat on the corner of her desk. "Peyton Kaplan dumped you that night. It was four in the morning when you came back to the estate after getting dumped."

Archie said, "He dumped you because you didn't have enough money for him."

"You went right past the studio and saw the lights on," Mac said. "That made it very bright."

She leaned towards him. "I told you the lights were off when I came back."

"According to Rachel's statement," Mac said, "she saw you going down the path toward the lake. She said she could see you because the lights were on. That was right after one o'clock, shortly after the time of the murder. While she was watching you leave, Greta came in from her swim in the lake."

"That's right." Rachel nodded her head quickly. "They were on when I saw you going down that path at around one o'clock."

"The lights were off when I found her the next morning," Neal said.

David said, "Since you were seen on the path after the time of the murder, and the lights were on, then they must have been turned off by someone else."

"Like whoever took the painting," Mac said.

Archie pointed out, "If the lights were off, you couldn't have found your way up the path to the house. It would have been too dark."

"That's right," Rachel said. "There's no other lights on that side of the estate."

Mac resumed, "When you were coming back to the main house, after getting dumped by Peyton, you looked inside the studio and found Ilysa Ramsay dead. Her painting was wrapped up for Victor Gruskonov to pick up."

Bogie said, "Which he couldn't do on account of him being dead."

Cameron said. "So you thought, 'Hmm, if I took this painting and sold it for a lot of bucks, then maybe I'll have enough money for Peyton to leave his wife for me.'" She shook her head. "Breaking the law for a man, especially a pig like Kaplan, is never a good plan."

David said, "Somehow, Rachel found out."

Rachel's eyes widened. "What do you mean I found out?"

The police chief recalled, "When I arrived at the scene, you and Susan were fighting. You told her to give it back." He cocked his head at her. "What did you want her to give back?"

Scott stepped away from her.

Neal gasped, "I remember you coming into the studio and screaming. Then, you ran back out."

"And confronted Susan," David said. "You've known all along that Susan took the painting but said nothing."

"Why didn't you say anything?" Scott demanded in voice so loud and sharp that it sounded like an explosion.

A smug grin crossed Susan's lips. "Haven't you figured it out yet, Scott? Rachel does have her price. I gave her half of what I sold the painting for, in exchange for her silence."

"Why?" Scott demanded from his wife to know. "You don't need money. I give you everything you ask for."

"I wanted some of my own…for a rainy day." She rolled her eyes. "And you'd be surprised how often it rains in my world."

"Especially when you stick it up your nose," Susan said.

"You bitch!" She delivered a slap across Susan's face with the speed of a whip.

Scott grabbed her around the waist to pull her back. While he held her back, Susan jumped out of her chair to slap Rachel repeatedly with both hands.

"Stop it!" David stepped between the warring women to push Susan back only to get slapped across the face.

"You never learn, boy." Bogie grabbed Susan by the wrist and twisted her arm to cuff her. "You're under arrest, Susan Dulin."

"For what? The statute of limitations is over for stealing the painting. You've got nothing on me."

"How about killing Ilysa?" Neal said.

"I didn't kill her. She was already dead when I stole the painting."

"For starters," Bogie said. "You're under arrest for assaulting a police chief." He nodded with his head in the direction of David, who was still rubbing his cheek.

Neal screamed at her, "You're also fired! While you're locked up, I'm throwing all of your stuff in the lake."

"Scott baby." Rachel reached for her husband's hand.

When she closed in, Scott stuck his hand in her pocket and pulled out a clear plastic bag containing white powder. "Susan wasn't lying. You have been sticking our money up your nose. I've been suspecting it for a long time, but didn't want to admit it." Shaking off her touch as if she held a contagious disease, he backed away from her. "Get away from me!" He turned to David. "Isn't this illegal?"

"It's called possession." David grabbed her by the wrist. "I'm afraid you're under arrest, Rachel."

"You can't arrest me." When she tried to pull away, David twisted her arm to slap the cuffs on her. "Don't you know who I am?"

"Not anymore," Scott said to her. "We're getting a divorce. You could have helped them find out who killed Ilysa years ago, but instead you took advantage of her murder to make money for what?" He shook the bag of powder in her face." "She was my stepmother! She was my family!" "

Neal asked, "Which one killed Ilysa? I want to know."

Rachel said, "I didn't kill anyone. All I did was blackmail Susan."

Mac told Neal, "Neither of them killed your wife."

"Who did?"

Mac turned around. "Greta." Not seeing her behind them, he asked, "Where did Greta go?"

Archie told them, "She was right behind us."

Sounding the charge, Gnarly ran from the office and into the kitchen. He took off so fast that he yanked the leash out of Archie's grip.

They heard a crash in the kitchen.

While David and Bogie secured Rachel and Susan to the desk chair, the rest of them rushed into the kitchen find to Greta at the knife block on the far side of the room.

"Stand back!" The housekeeper held the butcher knife to her own throat. "I'm going to do it! I swear!"

Seeing Gnarly approaching her, Archie screamed.

"Gnarly, come!" Mac demanded. He was surprised when the dog backed up to join him at his side.

"Greta," Neal asked, "you did it? You killed Ilysa? Why?"

"She was coming between us," Greta said. "From the beginning, she tried to split us up."

Not understanding, Neal shook his head.

"Like that time she had gone into my room when you first got married and she saw your pictures. I was in the parlor restringing my fiddle and she came in asking me all kinds of questions about us."

When she saw David gesture for Bogie to go around, Greta pressed the knife tighter to her throat. A drop of blood seeped from under the blade. "Don't move or I'll do it! I have nothing to lose! Now that I have hurt the only man I have ever loved—"

David gestured for Bogie to stay put. "We're not going anywhere, Greta. We don't want to hurt you."

"She told me that there was something wrong with me," Greta said. "She had no idea what it was to be devoted."

"You are devoted, Greta." Out of the corner of his eye, Mac saw Joshua and Cameron slip out from behind the crowd.

If I can move her over just a little bit, they can go out the back without her seeing.

"What happened when Ilysa found the pictures?" Mac slid over toward the strawberries.

As he had hoped, she followed him. "She said that she was uncomfortable with me working for them. Uncomfortable? Why should she be uncomfortable with me?" Tears rolled down her face. "I was here first. I know all about taking care of my family. Who is she to send me away?"

David said, "You were restringing your fiddle and you killed her."

"What?" Neal gasped. "What are you talking about?"

Archie patted his arm to quiet him.

Confusion crossed Greta's face. "But then, she came back."

Behind her, Mac saw Joshua and Cameron slip down the hallway leading to the back door.

Scott was shaking his head. "She came back?"

David whispered to him. "It's complicated."

"And then, Ilysa did the painting of when you had strangled her with the wire from your fiddle," Mac said.

"No, the painting didn't bother me." She shook her head. "I hid my pictures after we had the first fight and I killed her. Then, when she came back, I never said anything and neither did she and we got along great...until..."

They held their breath when Joshua emerged from around a corner behind her.

"Why did you kill her the second time?" David asked.

Tears soaked her face. "They started talking about traveling all over the world. She was going to take my man away from me. After everything I've done for him. I put off getting groceries yesterday to drive all the way up to Pittsburgh to kill that black-mailer. How many housekeepers will do—"

Joshua lunged at her from behind and grabbed the arm holding the knife. While he struggled to get the knife, Greta grabbed a second knife from the block and whirled around to swing it at him.

In the path of the knife, Cameron was stabbed in the upper chest. Even after being struck, she kept on going. With both hands on the hand with the butcher knife, she joined Joshua in slamming Greta's arm against the counter until it dropped from her grip.

In the fight, Greta kept hold of the second knife. She pulled it out of Cameron's chest and swung it again.

Before she could make contact, Gnarly's jaws clamped down on her wrist to jerk her back. Her wail reminded Mac of a screech owl that had awakened him many nights since his move to Deep Creek Lake.

Joshua retrieved the butcher knife from the floor and out of Greta's reach. "That's a relief." Only when he stood up, did he see Cameron slumped on the floor clutching her chest with blood flowing out from under her hand.

"Cameron!" Joshua dropped down onto his knees and grabbed her. His heart was beating hard against his chest wall while he watched her eyelids flutter. She was losing consciousness. "Stay with me, Cam. Don't leave me now. I'm not through with you yet."

"Emergency!" David called into his radio. "We have an officer down!"

Chapter Fourteen

It was the middle of the night before they gathered together at the Spencer police department to sort out the details.

After getting her superficial stab wound patched up at the hospital, Cameron made phone calls to her department to report on the Jane Doe, Victim Number Four and Lieutenant Sherry Bixby murders. Between solving two murders and getting wounded in the line of duty, she was due for some serious time off. She was planning to have a long talk with Joshua about that on the long drive home.

Meanwhile, David was up in his office returning a phone call from Special Investigator Harry Bush of the FBI.

After securing Rachel and Susan in their holding cells, which were directly across the hallway from George Scales's cell; Bogie broke out a bottle of whiskey that he kept in his bottom drawer for such occasions—the closing of a big case. Occasionally, they would hear Rachel and Susan arguing with each other.

"Wait until Peyton Kaplan gets picked up by the FBI for treason," Cameron said with a laugh. "The four of them can exchange prison stories."

"I still can't believe it." Neal downed the glass of whiskey that Bogie had served him and asked for another. "I always thought I was lucky to be surrounded by good people."

"I was fooled, too, Pop." Scott patted his father's shoulder.

Neal sighed. "At least your wife didn't get murdered weeks after the wedding and got replaced by another woman without you knowing it."

Scott signaled for Bogie to top off his glass. "No, my wife only jumped into a conspiracy to steal my stepmother's painting right over her dead body to buy coke."

Neal ran his hand over the top of his head. "My wife—wives—used me to steal government secrets from my own company." He looked over at Mac. "How can I continue as CEO?"

"They were very good at what they did," Mac offered.

"Actually, you aren't as big a fool as you thought." David came down the stairs from his office. "I was just talking to Harry from the FBI. They examined that smart chip that we uncovered from the painting. Do you know what it had on it?"

Joshua said, "The access codes for Hathaway's satellites."

David nodded his head. "That disk also had other stuff on it. Viruses. Big, bad, fatal viruses." He made an explosion noise and spread out his fingers. "Luckily, they ran a full scan of the disk before opening the files. It had the biggest baddest viruses in the IT world. Whoever opened the file on that disk would have wiped out not only their computer, but the whole network with no hope of ever repairing it."

With a sigh in her voice, Archie told Neal, "She did love you."

"I don't understand," Neal looked from one of them to the other. "Explain it to me. Ilysa or Fiona was selling her painting, which had these secret codes, but there was a virus on the disk."

Mac explained, "She was in love with you and wanted out. Victor Gruskonov wouldn't let her out. So, she decided to give them what they wanted, plus something extra—a bomb that would destroy their whole computer network."

"Rendering their computer system and the information she stole for them worthless," Archie said.

"Scales stated that she had fallen in love with you," David said. "She was blackmailing both him and Kaplan to resign as soon as the deal went down. She wanted to get rid of them, because they had betrayed you."

While they were talking, Archie and Tonya went into the backroom. They came out carrying Ilysa's painting between them. When Neal saw it, his eyes brightened only to become sad again.

"Would you like to take it home with you, Mr. Hathaway?" Tonya offered.

David said, "I talked to the prosecutor. You can take it with you, if you'd like."

"I don't know anymore." Neal slumped.

"Ilysa loved you, Dad." Scott patted his shoulder. "I have no doubt about that. She had said she painted her masterpiece for you. Remember when she unveiled the one in the foyer? How happy you were when she gave it to you?"

Whining, Gnarly patted his knee with his paw.

Neal stroked the top of the dog's head. "She did give the traitors a bunch of viruses. I guess she wouldn't have done that if she didn't love me." His eyes were moist when he told them, "Thank you. I think Ilysa…or Fiona…or whatever her name was would want me to have it."

Archie offered, "Greta loves you, too, in her own warped, homicidal way."

In spite of the murder of his wife being solved, it was with a sense of sadness that Neal Hathaway and his son carried the painting out with them when they left.

Silence filled the station while everyone reflected on the rich man who had discovered that almost everyone whom he had counted as friend and family, except his son, had betrayed his trust.

It was an unnerving discovery for anyone.

Joshua broke the silence to ask Mac, "How did you know it was Greta?"

"Don't feel bad." Mac grinned at him and Cameron. "It wasn't anything you missed. When Neal came to my place yesterday to tell me about your boss shaking him down, he said that he'd answered the phone because it was Greta's shopping day."

Archie gasped. "But the kitchen was filled with groceries today. She couldn't go shopping yesterday, because she had to drive up to Pittsburgh to kill Sherry who was—But how did she know about the call if she was out when it came in?"

"She hadn't left yet," Cameron said. "Greta mentioned that at the hospital. She'd come back inside the house, because she'd forgotten her coupons—"

"Coupons?" Bogie asked with shock in his voice. "She works for this big multi-millionaire and she shops with coupons?"

"Trying to save her boss money," she explained. "Greta was very loyal to Hathaway. Anyway, she had come back inside when the phone was ringing. They both picked it up at the same time, I guess. When she overheard Sherry blackmailing her man, Greta went into defensive mode."

Bogie said, "Too bad we didn't hear about her skinny dipping back then on the night of the murder."

"They didn't think anything about it because Greta does go skinny dipping on a regular basis," Archie said. "Rachel told us that last night."

"Unfortunately," Joshua said, "when witnesses are questioned at the time of a murder, they look for something out of the ordinary. Greta swimming naked in the lake didn't strike any of them as unusual. So, no one mentioned it."

"But it was unusual," Cameron said, "because that night, Greta wasn't simply skinny dipping, she was down there washing off the blood that she had to have gotten on her during the murder."

Bogie said, "But since neither Rachel nor Susan told us about it—"

"Because they both had their own agendas," David said with disgust in his tone.

"—we were never able to put it together."

Mac said, "You could have put it together if you had gotten a look at her room."

A search of Greta's living quarters revealed a closet filled floor to ceiling with pictures of Neal Hathaway that had been collected over the many years that she'd worked for him.

Archie grasped Mac's arm. "I guess living with a man—Taking care of him day in and day out, through the good and the bad, she began to think of him as more than a boss. She probably started fantasizing about the two of them, until she crossed the line into thinking it was reality. When Ilysa and Neal started planning to go away, Greta thought she was stealing her man away from her."

Bogie said, "And that was why she killed her. It had nothing to do with the painting—"

"She was too insane to even notice the symbolism in the painting," Mac said. "The gaunt expression on Greta's face, and the red tipped fingernails. Only to someone knowing the truth does it stand out. Unfortunately, Ilysa or Fiona didn't see that Greta was so crazy, that she was incapable of getting the message."

"Lurch, the maid of death." Cameron grimaced while tugging at the sling they doctors had given her in the emergency room. "I wish Fiona told me the truth back during Cartwright's trial. Then, she would still be alive and so would Bixby."

Joshua slipped his arm around Cameron's waist. "But then, we never would have met."

She smiled at him. "That makes this pain in my shoulder worth it." She kissed him. "Would you like to drive me home?"

"Home is over two hours away."

She kissed him on the ear. "I meant the Inn. It's getting late. I want to be there to warn the maid about Irving when she comes in to clean the room."

Joshua gestured toward the door. "Then, we have no time to waste."

After promising to meet Mac and Archie for lunch the next day, they left.

"Ah," Archie grasped Mac's hand into both of hers. "Did you see that?"

"See what?" Mac asked.

"They're actually glowing," Archie said. "They're in love. How sweet? Nothing is more romantic than falling in love over a juicy murder case." She tilted her head back and gazed up at him.

Mac bent over to kiss her, only to have Gnarly jump up to plant his snout on her cheek before him. "Gnarly, we need to get something straight. *I* get the girl in the end."

Epilogue

In the darkness of the night, with his eyes closed, Mac sensed her looking over at his motionless body. He breathed deeply so that Archie would think he was asleep. It worked. A moment later, she slipped out of his bed and tiptoed out of the room.

Mac counted to three before following.

In the sitting room, he saw her go into the bedroom on the other side of the penthouse and silently close the door. The granite floor was cold on his bare feet when he scurried across it to listen at the door on the other side. The sound of rushing air came from the room. It sounded similar to a hair dryer set on low.

What's she doing? Drying her hair? Her hair is too short to need a dryer.

Mac cracked the door open to peer inside with only one eyeball. The sound of air blowing became louder.

Her back to him, Archie sat on the bed while adjusting the knobs on what looked like an old fashioned radio set on the night table. A mask and air hose in her hand, she reached up to bring it down over her face and secure it in place with black elastic straps.

His curiosity taking over, Mac opened the door further.

When Archie turned around, he screamed when he saw her face covered with the mask and the hose projecting from her face to where it was attached to the box on the stand. She resembled something from a sci-fi movie.

The mask muffled her shriek. "What are you doing here?"

He pointed at the contraption. "What is that?"

She ripped the mask from her face. "What does it look like?"

"Hannibal Lector, that's what it looks like." The mask with the straps over her head did make her resemble the cannibalistic serial killer in the movie *Silence of the Lambs*.

"I know." Sobbing, she sank down onto the bed. "That's why I didn't want you to know."

Now you did it. When are you going to learn to think before blurting out what you think?

"Know what?" Mac came into the room. *Humor. That always works.* "Don't tell that you *are* Hannibal Lector."

"No."

"It can't be that bad."

When she didn't respond, he began to wonder. The sight of the mask, the hose, and machine. He assumed the worst. Even if he wasn't quite sure what that worst was. He prayed it didn't include death. "What is it?" He sat down on the bed next to her and took her hand. "Tell me."

She looked over at him. The shame he saw in her eyes made him tighten his grip on her hands. "I snore."

Mac waited for her to go on. When she didn't, he asked, "And…"

"Really bad."

"How bad? How about those little strips you buy—"

"They don't even start to help." She waved the mask at him. "In the college dorm, my snoring could be heard all the way down the hall. Talk about a non-existent sex life. When I slept, nobody slept. It wasn't until I fell asleep behind the wheel of the car that I went to a sleep clinic. I have sleep apnea. It's really bad. If I tried sleeping without this machine, my snoring would clear out the whole resort."

Mac went from wanting to hold and reassure her to wanting to toss her off the balcony. "Why didn't you tell me? I've been thinking that you weren't spending the night with me because I snored or punched or kicked. Now, I find out it's you."

"I told you it wasn't you."

"I would have believed you if you had told me that you snored and had to sleep with a vacuum cleaner strapped to your face."

"Would you have still wanted to spend the night with me if it meant sleeping with a vacuum cleaner hose?"

"If it meant you came with the vacuum cleaner, yes." Mac grabbed her by the shoulders. "Archie, I love you. I want you with me. If that contraption is part of the package, then I'll take it."

She threw her arm around him. Her mouth found his. With passion that felt as if was going to burst from her body, she held onto him. "You told me that you loved me."

He nodded his head. "I know."

"That's the first time you told me that."

"Is it?" he asked. "I didn't notice."

"I did." Her voice was husky. "Are you ready?"

Mac sucked in his breath. "Yes, I'm ready."

She slipped the mask on over her head and crawled under the covers.

Yep, she looks like Hannibal Lector. Holding his breath to keep from laughing, Mac slipped in next to her and wrapped his arms around her.

The sound of the air rushing through the machine took on a rhythm that soothed both of them to sleep.

Knowing that she would be there in his arms when he woke up, Mac drifted off to sleep. *She may be scary in bed, but I love her and she's mine.*

౭ ౮ ౜ ౯

Gnarly gave up on his master's return. He jumped up onto the bed, and dug with his paws and snout until he burrowed under the comforter. He stretched out the length of the king-sized bed and buried his head down under the pillows in the master bedroom of the penthouse suite at the Spencer Inn to fall sound asleep.

Ah, it's a dog's life.

The End

About the Author

Lauren Carr fell in love with mysteries when her mother read Perry Mason to her at bedtime. The first installment in the Joshua Thornton mysteries, *A Small Case of Murder* was a finalist for the Independent Publisher Book Award. *A Reunion to Die For* was released in June 2007. Both of these books are in re-release.

The Mac Faraday Mysteries take place in Deep Creek Lake, Maryland. The first two books in her series, *It's Murder, My Son* and *Old Loves Die Hard* have been getting rave reviews from readers and reviewers. *Shades of Murder* is Lauren's fifth mystery.

The owner of Acorn Book Services, Lauren is also a publishing manager, consultant, editor, cover and layout designer, and marketing agent for independent authors.

A popular speaker, Lauren has made appearances at schools, youth groups, and at conventions. She also passes on what she has learned in her years of writing and publishing by conducting workshops and teaching in community education classes.

She lives with her husband, son, and two dogs on a mountain in Harpers Ferry, WV.

Visit Lauren's websites at:

Website: http://acornbookservices.com/
      http://mysterylady.net/
E-Mail: writerlaurencarr@comcast.net

CHECK OUT THESE OTHER HIGHLY-ACCLAIMED

LAUREN CARR MYSTERIES!

The Mac Faraday Mysteries

IT'S MURDER, MY SON

An exciting mystery with plenty of intriguing and enigmatic characters, It's Murder, My Son is not a read that should be missed for mystery fans.

Reviewer: Margaret Lane
Midwest Book Reviews

What started out as the worst day of Mac Faraday's life would end up being a new beginning. After a messy divorce hearing, the last person that Mac wanted to see was another lawyer. Yet, this lawyer wore the expression of a child bursting to tell his secret. This secret would reveal Mac as heir to undreamed of fortunes, and lead him to the birthplace of America's Queen of Mystery and an investigation that will unfold like one of her famous mystery novels.

Soon after she moves to her new lakefront home in Spencer, Maryland, multi-millionaire Katrina Singleton learns that life in an exclusive community is not all good. For some unknown reason, a strange man calling himself "Pay Back" begins stalking her. When Katrina is found strangled all evidence points to her terrorist, who is nowhere to be found.

Three months later, the file on her murder is still open with only vague speculations from the local police department when Mac Faraday, sole heir to his unknown birth mother's home and fortune, moves into the estate next door. Little does he know as he drives up to Spencer Manor that he is driving into a closed gate community that is hiding more suspicious deaths than his DC workload as a homicide detective. With the help of his late mother's journal, this retired cop puts all his detective skills to work to pick up where the local investigators have left off to follow the clues to Katrina's killer.

OLD LOVES DIE HARD

The fast-paced complex plot brings surprising twists into a storyline that leads Mac and his friends into grave danger. Readers are drawn into Mac's past, meet his children, and experience the troubling relationships of his former in-laws. New fans will surely look forward to the next installment in this great new series.

Reviewer: Edie Dykeman
Bellaonline Mystery Books Editor

Old Loves Die Hard…and in the worst places.

Retired homicide detective Mac Faraday, heir of the late mystery writer Robin Spencer, is settling nicely into his new life at Spencer Manor when his ex-wife Christine shows up—and she wants him back! Before Mac can send her packing, Christine and her estranged lover are murdered in Mac's private penthouse suite at the Spencer Inn, the five-star resort built by his ancestors.

The investigation leads to the discovery of cases files for some of Mac's murder cases in the room of the man responsible for destroying his marriage. Why would his ex-wife's lover come to Spencer to dig into Mac's old cases?

With the help of his new friends on Deep Creek Lake, Mac must use all of his detective skills to clear his name and the Spencer Inn's reputation, before its five-stars—and more bodies—start dropping!

The Joshua Thornton Mysteries

A SMALL CASE OF MURDER
Independent Publisher Book Award Finalist!

A Small Case of Murder is a GRAND case of murder. Following a style, reminiscent of that of Lisa Scottoline, and David Rosenfelt, Lauren Carr in her debut novel A Small Case of Murder, delivers a powerful and strong detective- legal thriller that has all the makings of a Hollywood movie.

New Mystery Reader

Carr weaves an extraordinary story that is gripping and crafted at the highest level to entertain the reader with its touch familial centerpiece amidst evil and chaos.

Midwest Book Reviews

A Small Case of Murder is set in the quaint West Virginia town of Chester, where everyone knows everyone, and there is never a secret that someone doesn't know. In such an intimate town, how many suspicious deaths can be left unquestioned?

Following his wife's death, Joshua Thornton leaves a promising career in the U. S. Navy's JAG division to move across country with his five children into his ancestral home. While clearing out the attic they find a letter written to their grandmother post-marked 34 years ago.

In the letter, Lulu Jefferson wrote *"…Remember that dead body we found in the Bosley barn?…I saw him today…I went to talk to the reverend and there was his picture on the wall."* What dead body? His interest piqued, Joshua asks about Lulu and finds that in 1970 she died on the same day that she penned the letter implicating the pastor in an unreported murder. There is much more to this story than a 34-year-old letter. It's a 34-year-old mystery!

Today, a double murder has the whole town under a microscope. The state attorney general appoints Joshua special prosecutor to solve the crimes. In a small town where gossip flies as swiftly as a spring breeze, it is impossible to know who to trust. Asking simple questions about events long ago could prove to be deadly for Joshua and his family.

A REUNION TO DIE FOR

Lauren Carr writes with a flair that will not only keep you reading but also make you glad you didn't graduate with this class!
Romance Reviews Today

High school cheerleader Tricia Wheeler didn't make it to her graduation because a bullet went through her heart and killed her.

Twenty years later, a journalist is investigating Tricia's supposed suicide for a book. Suddenly, a second cheerleader is dead and the body count in the small West Virginia town continues to rise.

For Joshua Thornton, the case is personal. The reopening of the Wheeler case stirs up memories and feelings for a girl who died without knowing his true feelings for her. Now, the newly-elected prosecutor is challenged to use everything he's got to find out what had really happened to Tricia and stop the killing.

Coming Fall 2012!

Dead on Ice
A Lovers in Crime Mystery!